WRITER OF FUTURES

Other CV-2 Books by Raymund Eich

Stone Chalmers
The Progress of Mankind
The Greater Glory of God
To All High Emprise Consecrated
In Public Convocation Assembled

The Confederated Worlds
Take the Shilling
Operation Iago
A Bodyguard of Lies

Novels
The Blank Slate
New California
The Reincarnation Run

Short Novels
The ALECS Quartet
A Mighty Fortress

Collections
The First Voyages: The Complete Science Fiction Stories 1998-2012
Stage Separations: The Complete Science Fiction Stories 2013-2018

WRITER OF FUTURES

Raymund Eich

CV-2 Books • Houston

ISBN 978-1-952220-04-3
First CV-2 Books trade paperback edition: October 2020

Writer of Futures

Pase de un Día

The only displacement booth in San Lorenzo stood between the town hall and the church, where Calle Benito Juárez ended at Calle Progresso. The sky was pale in the east, but the sun had not yet risen over the Sierra Madre, when Chalo ran his hand over sleeping Berto's hair, kissed Adelina, and left their three-room house. Awakening birds chirped behind corrugated iron fences. Chalo's stomach felt hollow. He ignored it. Once he got to work, he would scavenge his morning meal from the previous day's pastries in the break room. His family needed the pesos he would save by doing so.

A few blocks from the displacement booth, he stopped at an intersection, looked left and right, and started across. A car horn blared, startling him, and he jumped back toward the corner. A big, old pickup running on the battery of its hybrid engine had come up behind him and now turned left across his path. The window was down and the driver showed a pudgy face with a scraggly mustache and a medium complexion. "Fucking Indian, you're so short I almost hit you!" The pickup's gasoline engine kicked in and the mestizo roared away, flinging pebbles of crumbling asphalt from his rear tires.

For a moment, a tiny flame of rage burned in Chalo's chest, and he hunched his shoulders and head over it. But rage at the mestizo would not build a better life for his son. He took a deep breath to snuff the smoldering emotion, then looked all ways before crossing the now-empty street.

Soon he passed the private school run by the gray-haired gringo couple. The gate stood ajar. From within came the sound of metal shutters rolling up and English spoken too fast for him to follow. *"Aiden wants us to come for dinner* Friday *to meet Nadezhda,"* said a woman's voice.

Friday. Did she ask her husband about the deposit deadline at the end of next week? Chalo counted days and hours and his wage, then multiplied them together. He would work every day but Sunday. He would have enough to pay the deposit and get Berto away from the incompetent teacher who slept all day at the government school. The Virgin had blessed Chalo with a son of great intelligence, but her blessing demanded Chalo provide Berto with every possible chance for his intelligence to thrive.

The sun had crested the Sierra Madre, but the church's shadow still covered the displacement booth when he arrived. The booth was a glass cylinder big enough for a family to stand together. Its door showed the laser-etched logo of Teletransportes Mexicanos. A ring of lights around the cylinder's top glowed green. When he opened the door, it swung so easily it seemed to push itself against his hand.

He took his trifold wallet from the inner pocket of his jacket. Old when Adelina had bought it at a flea market, the wallet's folds showed years of wear and the bottoms of the inner slots had long ago split, revealing the edges of his debit card and family photos. Mounted on the inner wall of the booth, opposite the door, were a card reader and a touchscreen. Chalo swiped his debit card and alphanumeric buttons appeared.

With one finger, he tapped out *u-s-d-a-y-p-a-s-s*, then *Introducir*. The next screen asked him to confirm the address and the fee. He touched *Sí*.

He flicked into another booth, twin to the first. He turned and stepped out into a broad, high-ceilinged room, crowded with people and echoing with a babel of voices. This place still made him nervous—he widened his eyes and jerked his head—but he had been through here a few days now and knew the routine. He'd flicked into one of a row of twenty booths standing along what guessed was the south wall. Five queues snaked around plastic railings and aimed for a far wall dominated by an immense United States flag. He went to the nearest queue and shuffled forward.

Most of the people around him were mestizos, with a few blacks and fewer Indians. Regardless of race, many were dressed, like him, in dark trousers and matching tee shirts bearing restaurant logos stitched on the front and displacement booth addresses printed across the back. Chalo heard multiple Spanish dialects; a nasal language that almost sounded like Spanish; and lilting English from some of the blacks. The languages of the other Indians were completely unintelligible. Did everyone from all the countries of the Americas who traveled to the United States on the *pase de un día*, the day pass, come through this border station?

When he was third in line from the checkpoint, Chalo slid his day pass from his wallet. The day pass' white face and red and blue accents were the only things to distinguish it from his debit card. Its English words made little sense to him–he could pick out *United States*, but little else. His printed name seemed to shift in three dimensions when he wiggled the card.

In front of him, a mestiza with a long nose, bunned hair, and a buttoned gray jacket turned her left shoulder toward the turnstile's scanner. *You should consider an implant instead of the card*, the gringo in the consular office had told him in a formal Mexico City accent. *It's more secure.*

Chalo had disregarded his words. If the consular official wanted him to take an implant, it must give the gringos some benefit over him. He understood cards. Even if the card were less secure, he would not lose it.

The turnstile snapped shut behind the mestiza, and the robot torso mounted to the turnstile snaked out its neck and turned its cold, peering face down to Chalo. He shrank from it, more than any morning since his first one through here. His heart thudded and his hand shook as he swiped his day pass through a card reader. *Blessed Virgin, Queen of Mexico, strengthen me....* His hand steadied and he stood a little taller. The robot was only a machine, no different than it had been on earlier days. The near-miss by the pickup in San Lorenzo had made him jumpy.

After a moment, the robot withdrew and a light shone green next to the turnstile. Chalo went through. Around him, a few people strode from the turnstiles toward a row of a dozen displacement booths. The booths looked the same as the one in San Lorenzo, except their doors bore the logos of different companies: Pelton Industries, JumpShift, FARcast, and Portkey Science, alternating in that order. All worked the same, he'd been told, and he'd discovered for himself over his first three days using the day pass. He hadn't yet used a JumpShift booth, so Chalo went to that company's nearest one.

The touchscreen held a swirl of pale blue dots on a darker blue background. It showed three white buttons, each bearing an icon: a red cross for a hospital, a blue shield for police, and a bright yellow dot racing around an outline of the United States. The border police. Going to any of those addresses would waste many of his twelve hours, or worse.

He moved his day pass to one end of the card reader slot. He had been told his debit card, because of its link to an account with a Mexican bank, would not work on the United States network. True or false, he had no need to experiment. He had to get to his job.

Chalo ran his card through the reader. The touchscreen's buttons wobbled and disappeared, and lines of text replaced them.

Destination/destino: The Shoppes at Indian Bend (NW service booth), Paradise Valley, AZ

Latest departure time/Última hora de la salida: 05:49:28 PM MST and the second ticked up to *29* by the time Chalo pressed the button *Yes/Sí*.

He flicked to work. Concrete block and hanging fluorescent lights defined a wide, empty concourse. Only a robotic mop-and-bucket occupied the space. Its mop slid back and forth over the concrete floor. Chalo turned to the right, heading for a glass door leading to the pedestrian mall. His black sneakers squeaked from the mop's damp residue.

From a large cargo booth behind him came the thudding sounds of its door locking and unlocking. Chalo glanced over his shoulder to see who, or what, had flicked in. From the booth rolled a robotic flatbed cart with a structure at the front for its batteries and its computer brain. Its cargo-handling arms were folded against the structure. On quiet tires, it went the other direction down the concourse, bound for the rear entrance of some boutique, bearing a stack of recycled cardboard boxes marked *Fabrique en France*.

The glass door opened for Chalo. The sky overhead was blue, but the pedestrian mall remained in shadow. Even so, the air was hotter and drier than home and would only grow more so during the day. Chalo began to sweat in his jacket as he followed the winding mall. Most of the shops he passed were closed, their dim interior lights and the dawn glow combining to illuminate window displays of men's suits, ornate jewelry, lingerie, golf clubs. Hidden loudspeakers played orchestral music and water splashed down statues of nudes in the fountains. In front of a perfume store, a sweet floral scent filled his nose.

A glow of lights spilled from a store's front windows onto pavers still in shadow. The sign overhead read *Riviera Maya Coffee & Chocolate Co.* Chalo went in.

A few customers, older men in polo shirts, sat scattered among the tables. They glanced up as Chalo passed, then returned their attention to their tablets. The door from the kitchen swung open, and Hernán approached with a black lacquered tray bearing a cappuccino and a chocolate croissant. He wore a black bowtie, a white jacket, and an imperious look. "You're late," he muttered in Spanish.

Alarmed, Chalo looked at the clock. "It's not yet six."

"That thing does not synchronize properly with the atomic clock. Señor Kaufmann is waiting." Hernán lifted his chin and went to one of the customers.

Through the kitchen, in the break room, Chalo quickly signed in on a touchscreen, moved his wallet to his back pocket, and hung his jacket. He found Kaufmann in his small, windowless office. "I'm sorry I am late, sir."

Kaufmann blinked over his reading glasses, then checked the time display on his tablet. "A few minutes until six. You have the proper attitude. Less than a week and you already understand how the better sort of gringos view time." Kaufmann himself looked like a gringo, pink-white skin and grizzled gray-brown hair, yet he spoke Spanish with an accent native to northern Mexico. It was not Chalo's place to ask if Kaufmann had grown up in Phoenix or Monterrey.

"Better to be five minutes early," Kaufmann went on, "than five minutes late. Remember that."

"I will, sir."

Kaufmann glanced at his tablet. "Three complete days, and you've done adequately so far. Your speed and quality metrics at bussing tables and helping in the kitchen are above average for a trainee."

Chalo had not known. Hernán had continually criticized his work. "Sir, thank you."

Kaufmann's face grew more serious, and he waggled a finger. "But you must not rest. You must approach every job with the idea of always improving. There are ten million Mexican men who would be above average trainees. Do you understand me?"

"I do, sir. I will always improve."

"And hang on to your day pass. I don't know why people squander their opportunity by losing it." He nodded toward the swinging doors to the kitchen. "It's time for you to get to work. Señor Halford has probably left for the golf course by now. His table needs bussing."

Chalo's duties gave the day a steady rhythm, and shifting sunlight and the flow and ebb of customers gave it a melody. He listened to the customers as he carried bins of dirty cups and plates to the robotic dishwasher in the kitchen. Though he understood few words, he wanted to learn all he could about the customers. It would help him improve at his job. And just maybe—a dream so close to impossible he could tell no one, not even Adelina; but thanks to the Virgin, it was possible enough—he might learn how to introduce Berto into their world.

First came doctors and nurses in blue scrubs, stopping at the take-away counter before their morning hospital shifts. Chalo heard the names of gringo cities, names just last week as mythic as El Dorado and Cibola, but now spoken by people a flick away from Seattle, Chicago, Los Angeles. Business people made up most of the crowd between seven and nine, men in three-piece suits, women in skirts and heels. They were often distracted, paying attention to conversations going through their earpieces.

"We absolutely cannot compromise any aspect of our handicraft certification," one businessman said, chopping the air with his hand to emphasize his words. *"If we falsely pass something as handmade and word gets out, our competitors will eat our lunch. No, I don't care what the elder told you. You tell him we can get the same goddamn rugs from the next village...."*

By late morning, the crowd had thinned. Most customers now were older women wearing tight faces and pantsuits modeled by mannequins in the windows of nearby boutiques. The women came in accompanied by blasts of dry, bakingly hot air.

"Yes, isn't this place marvelous? Far better than that robotic swill from the Seattle chain. The flour comes from nitrogen-fixing grains, certified fertilizer-free and they preserve so much habitat compared to the genetically unimproved varieties. The coffee and chocolate are fair trade. And all the employees are Maya from the Yucatan."

Maya from the Yucatan? Had she recently vacationed in Cancún? Chalo shrugged and took another bin of dirty plates to the kitchen. He fed the contents to the dishwasher while Hernán picked up a tray of coffees and pastries laid out by articulated robot arms mounted on tracks in the ceiling.

After a swell of customers stopping by on their way from their lunch hours back to their jobs, the crowd thinned again. Chalo ate a quick lunch of two hard-boiled eggs and a whey protein bagel while standing in a corner of the kitchen. Hernán's scowl lashed him into wolfing down his last bites and hurrying out to the dining room with his bin.

The next customer spike came around three: mothers relaxing for fifteen minutes before picking up children from school, groups of teenagers grousing about homework before pulling out their tablets to study together. Among the latter was a table of two boys. One, pure gringo, sported spiky blond hair and a narrow beard. An animated college logo looped on his tee shirt. His demeanor mixed the privilege of high status, guilt at the privilege, and an earnest desire to reconcile the two. The other was a slender mestizo in his early teens, in a school uniform of khakis and a blue polo. He gulped down one of the coffee cakes the older boy ordered, then looked bored. A tablet set down between them showed the logo of an agency or service called *Tutor For America*.

"Alfonso, describe the Thirtieth Amendment to the Constitution," the gringo boy said.

The younger boy frowned at his chocolate smoothie. *"Let's see. That's the one that gave Washington, D.C. two senators and a congressman?"*

The gringo boy's smile froze. *"That was the Twenty-ninth."*

"The Thirtieth. Something about citizenship?"

"That's right.... Citizenship and birthright...."

The younger boy reached for the tablet. *"Can I look it up?"*

"There are things its good to have in your mind and not just electronically."

"I can't remember. I give up."

The older boy sagged with an exhaled breath. *"The Thirtieth Amendment clarified the Citizenship Clause of the Fourteenth. Someone gets citizenship at birth only if both their parents are citizens or legal residents of the United States."*

"Why do I need to know this stuff? It's not on the SAT. My dad doesn't use this crap to run his restaurants. He'll give me a good job when I'm done with school. You're wasting my time."

The gringo boy blinked in confusion for a moment. *"I know it seems like a waste now... but your father worked to get your name in the lottery for tutoree slots and do you want to tell him you don't care?"*

The younger boy looked away and folded his arms. *"Fine...."*

"Now, where were—whoa!"

Chalo turned his head. A large white blur, then the smack of another body colliding with his. The bin slipped from his grip as he fell on his rear end. Cups and plates clattered on the floor, spilling dregs of coffee and crumbs of pastries. A cappuccino flowed around shards of porcelain. It had left tan drops on Hernán's pants when it fell.

The waiter glared down at Chalo. "You stupid fucking Indian!" His voice carried through the now-silent café.

Chalo's cheeks felt hot. "I'm sorry." He scrambled onto his knees and groped for broken cups and plates.

Motion in the corner of his eye resolved into Señor Kaufmann. "What's going on here?"

"This inept Indian didn't watch where he was going," Hernán said.

Chalo's face felt even hotter. What would this do to his numbers? Would Kaufmann fire him on the spot? He flung porcelain fragments into his plastic bin. Sharp slivers scratched his fingertips.

"That is not the full story," the gringo boy said in slow but correct Spanish. "Both men were looking the other way when they ran into each other."

Hernán clamped his lips together. He glowered at the gringo boy for a moment before it seemed he decided better of it. With a milder expression, he said, "I recall looking straight ahead, and even if I didn't, Chalo should watch for me, not I for him."

Kaufmann looked frustrated. "First we fix the problem. Later we find what went wrong and keep it from happening again. You lost an order, Hernán? Replace it and comp the customer. Then help Chalo clean up if he isn't done by then."

Hernán looked sullen, then stalked off to the kitchen. Chalo picked up more shards of cups and plates and mopped up spilled coffee with a tea towel.

"*What did you say?*" the younger boy asked the gringo.

"*That it wasn't the busboy's fault.*" His eyes narrowed and his lips parted, as if he wanted to ask a question.

"*What's that look? You think I'm supposed to speak Spanish?*"

In the gringo boy's face, guilt overwhelmed privilege. "*No, no, of course not. Let's get back to work. Where were we, Alfonso?*"

"*You know I want to be called Al....*"

Chalo hurried to the kitchen with a full bin. Hernán passed him and gave a cold stare. Chalo hustled to the trashcan and shook the broken pieces out of the bin. A cold feeling washed through him. He had lost his job. He had failed Berto. He–

He would do his best, even if today was his last day here. Chalo stood a little straighter and returned to the dining room.

Walking near the table with the two boys, someone said, "Señor."

Was Kaufmann still about? Chalo hurried on.

"Señor!" It was the gringo boy, and he called for him. Chalo stopped and faced him, but, uncertain how he could respond, said nothing.

"Your wallet." The gringo boy pointed to the floor near the collision site. It must have fallen from Chalo's pocket when he'd landed on his rear end. Minutes ago and he hadn't noticed!

Chalo hesitated, then set down his bin and picked up the wallet. Still barely intact, but it seemed to be in one piece. Wobbly with relief, he shoved it into his hip pocket and bobbed his head at the gringo boy. "Gracias." He tried his English. "Thank. You."

"You're welcome." The gringo boy looked pleased with himself. Chalo picked up the bin and hurried to the nearest unbussed table. A few words from the younger boy reached him when he was still close enough. *"Five billion third worlders want jobs in America, and the owner can't find one who speaks English?"*

Five o'clock brought the last burst of customers, as the after-work crowd filled the tables around the two boys. Chalo eyed the clock. He would have about twenty minutes from the end of his shift until his day pass would expire. Enough time, but he couldn't dawdle.

At five-thirty, Chalo tossed his last load of dirty plates to the dishwashing robot, then went into the break room. Hernán listened sullenly to Kaufmann. "...That's all, Hernán."

"I'm going to take my break now." Hernán turned and scowled at Chalo, then went into the kitchen and turned for the service doors leading to the rear concourse.

Chalo shuffled closer to the office. "My shift is over, Señor Kaufmann. I must return home while my daypass is good. If you want me to return tomorrow."

Kaufmann frowned. "Why would I not? The spilled plates? Accidents happen and you're within tolerances." He tapped his fingers on his tablet. "Let's keep it that way. Until tomorrow." He chopped the air with his hand as a businesslike wave. Chalo tapped his code on the wall-mounted touchscreen to clock out for the day, then hurried toward the displacement booth.

Heat baked him less than two meters from the front doors. He walked a few minutes toward the late afternoon sun, passing the two boys in the window of a teen clothing store. Chalo squinted, and moved his jacket from arm to shoulder in hopes of finding a spot where it would trap less heat against him. Opening the door to the service concourse gave him a relief. The service concourse lacked air conditioning, but being windowless, was slightly cooler than the outside.

He went in the displacement booth and dug his wallet from his pocket. Open it up and—where was his daypass?

Chalo rifled through his debit card and his family photos, then again. If it wasn't there.... He must have put it in the wrong slot after flicking in that morning. He checked the currency slot and found only his few, worn dollars and pesos. In one of his pants pockets? His jacket pocket? He plunged his hands into all in turn. No daypass.

Panic climbed up the inside of his chest. If he'd lost his daypass, he would have to flick to the U.S. border guards. They would send him home, but he would lose any chance for another daypass. A billion men could be above-average trainees, but his son would languish another year in the government school, and that year might be enough to smother Berto's intelligence forever–

Breath deeply. Retrace your steps. Your wallet never left your pocket, except when you collided with Hernán.

He checked the time on his phone. About fifteen minutes until his daypass expired. He ran out of the concourse. His feet pounded down the sun-baked mall. Chalo veered to avoid a pair of tall gringas peering down their narrow noses at him, which brought into his view the gringo boy and the one being tutored.

A sudden idea made him stumble to a stop. A mix of English and Spanish spilled from his mouth. "Señor, favor, please, mi wallet, mi daypass, pase de un día, is fall out–"

The gringo boy took a moment to recognize him. "Oh, you're the busboy," he replied in Spanish. "You lost your daypass? It was in your wallet when you collided with the waiter? It looks like a credit card, yes?" His wince showed sympathy. "I'm afraid I didn't see it anywhere on the floor in the café."

Chalo's face slumped. Frustration tightened his mouth and lowered his brows. He glanced at the mestizo boy. Had this one seen something? He would have to tell. By the Virgin, Chalo would make it clear he had to tell. Chalo stood as tall as he could and drew up to eye level on the boy. Unease panged him as he looked the boy straight in the face. "Did you see it?" Chalo asked in Spanish.

"*What?*" came the reply, in English. The boy grew surly. "No hablo español."

"*Did you see his daypass fall out of his wallet?*" the gringo boy said.

"*Why would I care enough to look? No, I didn't see it.*"

The gringo boy winced in more sympathy. "Neither of us saw it." He looked thoughtful for a moment. "But the waiter passed by the spot soon after everything happened. He might have noticed something."

"Thank you," Chalo said in Spanish. Time was too tight to bother with English. He ran down the mall. Sweat stuck his shirt to his back. The air conditioning inside the café made him shiver.

He went to the tables near where he'd fallen. Customers frowned and he barely noticed as he peered around chair and table legs for a glimpse of white with red and blue accents. Nothing. Frantic, he called to another busboy, "Have you seen Hernán?"

"No." The other busboy kept filling his bin.

"He's on break," said Kaufmann. Chalo's eyes widened in alarm. Kaufmann would not want to be bothered with his problem. "Why do you need him? You should be on your way home."

Again, the Virgin helped Chalo stand straight. "I lost my daypass. Sir, it was in my wallet, I swear to you it was, I wouldn't lose it for a stupid reason, but it must have fallen out when I fell down after running into Hernán and I want to ask if he saw it."

Kaufmann frowned, but Chalo soon realized, not at him. "He should be back from break by now. Come with me." Kaufmann went to the kitchen without a glance behind him. Chalo hurried after. The service doors slid apart and Kaufmann led the way onto the concourse.

"That fucking thing's got five minutes till expiration," said a high male voice in Spanish. "I'd be super lucky to find a hoodlum who needs it to make a getaway. Twenty dollars."

"Alright, I'll take–" Hernán broke off. The other, a slender barrio boy, froze wide-eyed. The barrio boy recovered first; he snatched Chalo's daypass from Hernán's hand and ran down the concourse toward the service booths. His boots thudded on the concrete and his pants slipped down his backside.

"Thieving son of a whore!" Kaufmann shouted as he ran after him. Chalo ran too, but with his shorter legs, fell further behind with each step. The barrio boy looked over his shoulder. The white of his eye stood stark against his skin and black hair. As he looked back at them, he lost his footing and stumbled. Kaufmann tackled him. The barrio boy thudded to the floor, breath whoofing out and the daypass skittering from his hand.

"Take your daypass and go, Chalo," Kaufmann said. "I'll deal with the police."

"Yes, sir." Chalo reached for the card, then gave a look back at Kaufmann and the barrio boy. In the distance, near the service entrance to the café, Hernán was out of sight.

"Go! I need you back here in the morning. It will be a busier day than usual, with one less waiter on staff."

Chalo nodded and ran down the concourse to the displacement booth, muttering an Ave Maria as the daypass dug into his palm.

AffEctive Disorder

The biotech company occupied a glass-and-steel lowrise in the manicured pine forests of Houston's northern suburbs.

Albert Jimenez climbed out of his car at the front doors. While it parked itself, he entered a reception area. Terrazzo clacked underfoot, and chrome letters float-mounted and backlit on a curving wall spelled out AffEctive Technologies.

Why the italics? he mused, while he waited for Rachel Nguyen, the company's general counsel.

Pantsuit, black hair to the shoulder, and an expression on the severe side of the knife-edge professional women had to walk between femininity and authority. Albert shook her offered hand. Smooth skin, warm, not moist. "I'm glad to match a face to your reputation," she said. "Let's go to my office."

In Nguyen's office, file folders lay on her desk like sedimentary strata, and on the credenza, a slideshow of family photos filled the unused monitors. The windows showed pines and the harsh light of a Texas summer day. "Have a seat," Nguyen said, and waved at a chair facing the desk. The leather squeaked as Albert shifted his weight. Nguyen sat in a webbed ergonomic chair on her side of the desk and regarded him.

Half Albert's business came from litigation-support investigations, a euphemism for parties in lawsuits seeking dirt on their opponents. "What's the case?"

"A few months ago, did you hear about the suicide of Patricia Jameson?"

"I follow the news." An heiress with psych problems. Houston had a thousand of them.

"One thing that hasn't been reported is that she was a test subject in a Phase III trial of our device, AffEctor."

"Device?" Albert asked. "It's not a drug?"

"Not as such. Our device is a tiny biochemical factory—about a cubic millimeter in size—implanted in the brain. It contains an engineered strain of the bacterium *E. coli*. The bacterium name is where the marketing team came up with the typographical trick in the company's." She wrinkled her nose to express her opinion.

Albert frowned. "Wait, *E. coli*? People get sick from exposure to it."

She raised her palm. "Our scientists could explain it more fully. I'll summarize. We've knocked out enough genes to make it harmless. Our *E. coli* can't live outside the device, so there's no risk of a gastroenteritis outbreak from them."

She flicked the air with two fingers. "Enough of what they cannot do. Here's what they can. We engineered them to produce serotonin and endorphins. Those are mood-elevating compounds naturally found in our brains. Over twelve hundred people have used it up to an including our Phase III. Jameson's was our first suicide."

"Her family filed the suit?"

"Her husband. Phillip Jameson. He's alleging wrongful death due to negligence. He wants millions, and so do our outside counsel to defend against him. Which is where you come in."

Albert nodded. Hiring him to unearth Phillip Jameson's secrets would cost AffEctive a tiny fraction of the prospective legal fees and damages.

Nguyen went on. "The worst of it is he helped us get started. His firm, Mizukami and Choudhary, works with biotech start-ups. He asked to get his wife into the trial."

"That sounds irregular."

"It's uncommon," Nguyen said. A pained look formed on her face. "Your fee is three thousand a day?"

He looked apologetic. "Thirty-five-hundred. The euro's been strong lately. Plus expenses."

Nguyen quirked her mouth, then sighed. "From what I hear, you're worth it. Beam me your contract."

A few moments later she swiped a stylus across her phone, then beamed back an electronically signed copy. Albert glanced at the swirls of her name on his phone's screen, then asked, "Do you have a file started on Phillip Jameson?"

Nguyen nodded. "Yeah, it's...." She turned to her computer, nudged the mouse. A legion of icons held formation on the screen. A few clicks. "Here you go."

"Thanks." His phone bonged with receipt. He swiped through the first few pages. A few general notes on Jameson. Not much to start with.

Every thing they left out means more work for you, part of him thought as he went to his car. From the moment it opened its doors for him, shame at the thought dogged him the entire drive home.

The next day found him at a neighborhood pool across town from his house. The diving board thudded, and a young boy shrieked and splashed in, knees drawn to his chest. "Thanks for meeting with me, Maria," Albert said.

"It's no bother—I haven't seen you in ages," she said. Solitary grays streaked her dark brown hair and she rubbed sunscreen into thickened thighs. Men had it lucky, he mused. *At first glance, only our spirits embrittle and sag with age.*

"How's private investigation?" she asked.

He shrugged. "Better than HPD."

She arched her eyebrow. "What does freelancing give you that we didn't?" A faint emphasis rode her tone. He read it to mean she was between relationships again. Her brown eyes looked plaintive, and her gaze wandered over his face, then away.

He ignored her subtext. "Less paperwork. Now what—"

Shouts came from a corner of the pool. Maria leaned forward in her deck chair. A knot of eight-year-olds, her son among them, splashed and grappled. It took her a moment to loosen her grip on the arms of the deck chair. "I'm sorry, you were saying?"

"What can you tell me about Patricia Jameson's suicide?"

She crossed her arms over the stretched spandex waist of her bathing suit. "A lot. But what's in it for me?"

"Credit at the favor bank."

"That's all?" She put on a pout.

"There might come a time when you could use some off-the-books help with an investigation."

She thought about that as a cloud scudded in front of the sun.

"You saw plenty like them," Maria said. "Her husband called 911 about nine-thirty that night to report his wife was dead, apparently suicide. My homicide partner and I got to the house after a patrol car and an ambulance."

"Was he at home when she killed herself?"

"He said he had just returned from work and found her body. A law firm downtown, Matsu-something—"

"Mizukami and Choudhary?"

"That's it. We checked his whereabouts. His ID card showed he'd been in his office building all day, and according to the traffic control transponder in his car, it dropped him off that morning and parked in a garage outsdie downtown all day until he returned home."

"So he's clear."

Maria nodded. "The scene itself was so damn pathetic. One of those big houses on upper Kirby, you know, fifty feet off the street and they don't light up the front yard at night."

"Poor little rich girl," Albert said.

"Yeah, like she could have problems. A husband, no kids, tens of millions in the bank." She shut her eyes. "At the scene, the victim was slumped over on the couch. Silk kimono and underwear, her sphincters relaxed. Woke up and killed herself, it looked like. The coroner put time of death at about two PM."

"Overdose?" The most common means of suicide for an upper-class woman.

Maria nodded. "We found an empty bottle of sleeping pills on the table, and a spilled bottle of cognac on the floor." She shook her head. "How can someone who spends twelve hundred bucks on a bottle of liquor need to kill themselves?"

"How was her husband?" he asked.

"Oh, he was a son of a bitch. He plastered this shocked look on his face, but it was fake. He was glad to be rid of her. And he asked all these questions, was it murder, was it assisted suicide?"

"That's odd." Patricia Jameson had a history of mental illness; surely her husband would have assumed the simplest explanation.

"Yeah, it was so plainly suicide. No note, but there usually isn't. No phone calls in or out; no sign of forced entry or struggle; no one seen by the neighbors or the home security system."

Two girls in baggy waterproof *chadors*—Iranian? Pakistani?—climbed out of the pool and padded to the drink machine. The July sun lifted their footprints off the concrete deck.

"What about her medical implant?" Albert asked.

"Medical implant? Oh, yeah, I remember now. Jameson started talking to himself, stuff like, 'I got her in that trial because I trusted AffEctive. It was supposed to work. Did it fail?' I thought he was talking about a drug until I got the coroner's report. Damn, that's frightening, putting bacteria in your brains to shit out some drug."

"Did Jameson talk about lawsuits?"

"After a few minutes, yeah, he started ranting. 'Were they lying about the safety and efficacy? What were they thinking, screwing with me? I'm a lawyer.'"

Albert scrawled notes on his phone. If Jameson had a lawsuit in mind before his wife's body reached the morgue, AffEctive's defense could argue it as a sign of no emotional distress, meriting reduced damages. But Jameson would trot out enough expert witness psychologists to cloud the jury's mind. Not Albert's problem. He gathered the information; how the attorneys used it justified them earning in an hour what he made in a day.

He sounded her out for more information, but got nothing useful. "Thanks for your time, Maria." He stood.

Her gaze held him. "I'm not looking for something that we both know isn't there, but would you want to get together over drinks sometime? Some things you can only talk about with another cop."

"I'm an ex-cop."

"Getting rid of the badge didn't change you," she said. She unfurled her fingers toward him. "Just a drink."

Her agenda seemed clear—just a drink, leading to sex, followed by enough other booty calls to keep him coming back indefinitely. *Christ, you've gotten more cynical than I recall*, part of him thought.

"I know what you mean about the badge," he said. "Yeah, a beer, sounds good. I'll give you a call when this case cools down."

"Sure." Her smile didn't reach her eyes.

Albert spent the evening in the pale glow of the monitors, hunting the public and semi-private webs for data on the Jamesons. Small wonder Jameson felt relieved the night of his wife's death. Patricia Jameson had been the only child of John Allocatelli, a storage-peripherals tycoon around the turn of the century. (Two hundred megabytes in twenty cubic centimeters had once been impressively dense. Albert shook his head). Allocatelli had the savvy to sell out to a competitor before Moore's law smashed his business model.

Business savvy, and ill luck. The Allocatellis died in a Zapatista guerrilla attack on their resort on Cozumel, and left Patricia an orphaned nineteen-year-old multimillionaire. Somehow she'd kept her assets intact against all the distant relatives and financial advisors who must have come out of the woodwork to "help" her manage her inheritance. Kept intact so that now, between forty and fifty million dollars' worth of stock in computer hardware companies, passed to Jameson. Even today, that was a lot of money. How much more could he need? Oh, no, the lawsuit was about *principle*, bankrupt Aff*Ec*tive so they can't do this to anyone else. Lawyers with principles. Albert sniffed out a breath.

Patricia Jameson had received treatment for unipolar affective disorder—call it depression, for Christ's sake—for the two decades since her parents' death. Dozens of medications, multiple psychotherapists, hospitals, experimental treatments.... She had been a money machine for the Houston psychiatric community. Small wonder she was never cured.

His web searches dug up more dirt on Jameson. A couple of speeding tickets, an IRS audit. Not enough. He went through an anonymizer to try remotely logging into the database of Mizukami and Choudhary, but security stonewalled him. Three failed attempts to login with Jameson's likely username and common, simple passwords timed out his IP address for ten minutes.

Albert spent a while surfing the gray net, chatting up shady characters with handles like 'Rain Dog' and 'Schwarzritter' before he found what he needed. He bought time on a botnet from a cracker called 'Supervato,' and fired it up. The clock ticked while bot-ridden enslaved computers sent a steady stream of login requests to Mizukami and Choudhary's server from IP addresses around the world.

Albert took off his glasses, rubbed his eyes. Kalyani Krishnamurthi sang a torch song over the audio stream. The botnet could hit it lucky any minute, or could take days to brute-force every possible password combination.

No harm leaving the botnet running, even if sensitive data at Mizukami and Choudhary could be cracked by old-fashioned means.

Around nine the following night, Albert wheeled a cleaning cart to Jameson's corner office. He wore faded jeans, earphones piping in Tejano music—accordions and a man crooning about *mi corazon*—and a blue smock with "Jésus – Garcia

Sanitation" on the nametag. Two benjamins to the shift foreman had gotten Albert his disguise. He turned on the motion sensors he had clipped to the outside of the trash bag hanging from the cart. In his ear, beeps sounded over the music when he circled the cart on his way into the office.

Jameson had left the lights on. Apparently he was old-school enough to prefer paper. Piles of trifold folders, legal-sized and the color of unfinished pine, lay on the cherry desktop, their twins mirrored in the picture windows. Volumes of patent procedure and regulatory law stood in the bookcase. The computer screen was dark, but a green light glowed on the monitor. Albert picked up the trashcans and walked toward the door. Beeps rang in his ears. He dumped the trashcans' contents into the bag on his cart, then glanced up. A plump woman in a blue smock, fifty feet down the hall, pushed a cleaning cart away from him and toward the elevator lobby. Albert dismounted his vacuum cleaner from the cart and reentered the office.

Most people assumed security threats came from cyberspace, and paid semi-competent hackers to defend their web pages and servers. Yet those same people would leave their password on a notepad in their desks—

He pulled on rubber gloves and pushed the vacuum with one hand while the other opened the drawers. Hanging files; an organizer tray with pens, a ruler, a pad of sticky notes—

Blank. Top sheet, second sheet, last sheet, bottom. Albert set the pad back in place. A thought hit him. He lifted the tray, and for a moment forgot to push the vacuum.

A torn piece of paper held a twelve character string of letters, numbers, and symbols. That was the second most interesting thing in the drawer. A photo of a woman stared up at him. She looked to be in her late twenties, sitting on her ankles and cupping a handful of blond hair over her ear. She wore a coquettish grin and a lacy scarlet ensemble out of a fetishist's dream: bra, panties, stockings, garter. At the bottom, overlaid yellow digits said 03-03-37, over a month before Patricia Jameson's suicide. Albert fished his phone from his pocket and recorded both the photograph and the twelve character string, then put the tray back in place and shut the drawer.

It wasn't Patricia Jameson in the photo, for damn sure. A program could match a name to the face, and whatever the name, it wasn't going to belong to a casual acquaintance. If AffEctive's lawyers could stack a jury with women, Jameson would be in trouble. With luck, Jameson would settle on favorable terms. It took a few seconds for Albert to realize he'd pushed the vacuum over a patch of carpet for the eighth time.

A great night, and it might get even better. He let the vacuum stand alone, roaring, and crossed to Jameson's computer. The CPU's power was on. Albert nudged the mouse, and a login screen dawned on the screen. The username was already filled in.

Albert typed in the password. Moments later, Jameson's desktop appeared.

Albert dug in his pocket for a flash drive, ready to attach it to the computer. Where to start looking for sensitive files? God knew what was on the M&C system, but hopefully Jameson would hide his skeletons on his own hard drive and not the firm's server—

His earphones beeped, again, again. Someone walked down the hall. Oh shit. Maybe someone going into another office? The beeps continued. Albert took a step away from the computer, then realized the monitor still showed Jameson's desktop. Dammit! Turn it off and hope Jameson wouldn't notice. Albert's gloved finger poked the power button, and the monitor blackened. Albert scampered to the vacuum.

Be what he expected. Albert pushed the vacuum and bobbed his head to the music. His heart thudded, and his mouth tasted dry. Chill. Then he realized his rubber gloves were still on.

Jameson's reflection appeared in the window. He had tousled blond hair and craggy cheeks, and a gold pin lifted the knot of his tie away from the placket of his shirt. He crossed to the desk, searched through a stack of folders, took a handful, and left. Not a word to Albert. Not even a glance.

Albert breathed deeply for a few moments. Jameson had better not have forgotten something else. He returned to the computer, slid in the flash drive, and copied over as much of Jameson's hard drive as would fit.

Albert got home around one, and plugged the phone and the flash drive into his computer. He opened FaceInTheCrowd and had it search for matches to the woman in the photograph. He tried Houston first; wouldn't take but a few minutes. Albert started the run and backgrounded it, then gave Patterner the harder job of analyzing the files from Jameson's hard drive. All chaff, probably, but it had to be done.

Go to bed? He could read the name of Jameson's mistress in the morning, but he felt too keyed up. He went to the fridge and cracked open a Soweto Stout. A random preview from the cable company's server showed clips from the Tigres-Pumas Mexican soccer match, tomorrow's Nikkei ticker, and Melissa Tungsiri-pat's Thai food show *There Once Was a Chef from Near Phuket*. He settled on the soccer match and sipped his beer.

The computer bonged. Albert shut the TV off and entered the den. Onscreen, the blonde appeared in a driver's license photo, pendulous shadows hanging beneath her ears. Lori Schleiermacher, address in a zone of yupscale townhouses between Binz and Southmore, her age twenty-six, an organ donor.

Albert opened another instance of Patterner, this one wgetting online search results to find connections between her and Jameson. He turned off the monitor and sat for a moment in the darkened room, cold air tumbling out the vent, his toes scratching the coiled nap of the carpet. Another beer? Why, so he could feel hungover in the morning? Instead he climbed into bed and stared at the ceiling until his eyelids finally drooped.

By the next morning, Patterner had bound Schleiermacher to Jameson. They had met at a health club a year and a half before, and in that time had averaged three phone calls a week between her townhouse and his office. Her debit card had purchased two glasses of wine during an opera intermission; Jameson's had purchased two tickets for the performance. In January, two days before Jameson's birthday, she bought a titanium putter, but she had never golfed.

Albert daydreamed of her testimony. Jameson loathed his wife, had planned divorce for months before her suicide. Albert typed notes, when the phone rang. Who was calling so early? Wait, it was nearly eleven. He picked up.

"Mr. Jimenez?"

"Ms. Nguyen, hello. How may I help you?"

"We wanted to see how you were doing."

"Pretty good." He smiled and said, "Jameson's had a mistress for over a year." Nguyen huffed out a breath. "Really?"

"Yeah."

"That helps our case. What do we know about her?"

"Mostly name and address at this point. I'm still reeling stuff in. I'll prepare a report on her within the next couple days."

"I'm looking forward to it," Nguyen said. "We show him up as an adulterer and no jury will buy damages for emotional distress, at least. Our lawyers will love this. Anything else?"

"Not yet, but let's see—" He dragged and clicked until the Patterner window popped up. Though he couldn't mention the source of the files, he could inform Nguyen of the Patterner run's results. He scrolled. "Here's some names. His wife Patricia, Lori Schleiermacher—the mistress—Carter White—some damn attorney—Richard Wang, Steffani Lockhart—"

"Wait. Richard Wang?"

"W-A-N-G. Know him?"

"We have a Richard Wang on our staff," she said.

"Is he an attorney?"

Nguyen said slowly, "He's a tech."

"Was he involved in signing Patricia Jameson up for the trial?"

"No! I mean, no, that's not his job. He's a tech. —Why was he talking to Jameson?"

"I don't have that. Yet. I'll call you back."

"I want to hear as soon as you find out something on Jameson and Wang," she said. "Day or night. I'm serious, don't delay a second. I have to go." A dial tone buzzed in Albert's ear. After a second he cradled the handset.

Nguyen was spooked by Wang's involvement. Why? He called up the files of Jameson's that mentioned Wang and began to read.

Jameson's notes about Wang sounded cryptic—"RW preps" (what did Richard Wang prepare?), and fragments of names that turned out to belong to banks in the Caymans and Slovenia. Albert ran Supervato's icebreaker on the banks, the phone companies, and the credit bureaus, to glean data to link Jameson and Wang. When he checked back a few hours later, blood rushed in his ears as he clicked through the documents.

He picked up the phone, spoke as soon as Nguyen said hello. "Jameson and Wang talked by phone about a dozen times between last October and the week after Patricia Jameson's suicide."

Nguyen took a moment to reply. "We signed people up for the trials in October. Implantation happened early November."

"Jameson also paid Wang."

"I want to know, and I don't want to know. How much?"

"Five and a half million, two last October and the balance after the suicide," Albert said. Nguyen's silence, and the look on her face, hinted at the answer to his next question. "What did Wang do?"

"He was in charge of the assembly of AffEctor units for our trial. He oversaw the workers, and he also did QC on the *E. coli* strains we used. As well as the ones we didn't use. Shit!"

"That sounds serious?"

Her expression showed she realized she'd talked over his head. "In our freezers, we've got stocks of a bunch of strains. Most are low- or non-expressors of serotonin or endorphins or both. In place of our efficacious strain, he could've implanted into the unit substituted another one, say to up serotonin a little and depress endorphins all to hell. That's a combo that can lead to suicide. Wang could've done that and no one else would've known."

"They killed Patricia Jameson," Albert said. As surely as if they'd poisoned her. He remembered what Maria had said and shivered. Damn, it was frightening, to monkey with things that made us human.

"We're talking about more than settling out of court, aren't we?" Nguyen asked.

"We have to call HPD."

Nguyen sniffed out a breath. "Do it. I want these bastards nailed to the wall."

Four days later, Albert waited for Maria at the bar of a business casual restaurant on 290 near her subdivision. Outside, through the horizontal slats of the blinds, traffic crawled outbound on the freeway. Albert sipped his beer, under a faux-distressed farm-road sign and TVs tuned to soccer and baseball. Halfway through his glass, Maria shuffled in. He waved, and she weakly smiled.

After the hellos and the placing of her order, he asked, "What's the scoop?"

"This case is breaking my heart."

"Tell me."

The waitress came over with Maria's daiquiri. "Jameson and Wang are guilty as sin, but we can't get them to trial."

"Shit." Albert stared at his beer and shook his head. "I know my evidence was a little shaky—"

"The judge gave us arrest and search warrants. That's when things fell apart."

"How?"

"During the interrogation Jameson's lawyer quoted the damn statutes at us. 'The Texas Penal Code,'" she said in a poor imitation of an East Texas drawl, "'defines murder as intentionally or knowingly causing the death of an individual.'"

"But—" Jameson didn't shove the pills down his wife's throat. Encouraging formation of a mental state wasn't the cause of death. "No, wait, there's another clause, about intent to cause serious bodily injury and committing an act dangerous to human life—"

"I worked a week of late nights with an assistant DA. I had to leave Eddie with my half-sister, the tatted tramp. Murder, manslaughter, criminally-negligent homicide—the assistant DA told us Jameson's lawyer would get all disputational about what all the words mean. He did."

"What about aiding suicide?"

"Jameson didn't attempt to aid her suicide attempt. He didn't put the pills in her hand."

Albert shook his head. There must have been something to charge him with. "The AffEctor unit! Tampering with a consumer product!"

"Maybe," Maria said. "Problem there is it's only a felony to tamper with a product such that that product will probably cause bodily injury or death. But the unit didn't cause her death, did it? That double handful of pills she swallowed is what did."

Albert stared at his beer. "Shit."

"Let alone that we don't have any proof," Maria said. "After the autopsy, guess who the unit got returned to."

"AffEctive?" Maria glumly sucked on her daiquiri straw. "Worse than that."

"Attention Richard Wang." Albert couldn't say another word.

"But even if we could prove it," Maria said, "what've we got? Here's what the assistant DA said. If people are responsible for their actions, then the victim's suicide was entirely her choice, and Jameson walks. And if she wasn't responsible for her suicide, just a puppet of brain chemicals, then Jameson was a puppet of his brain chemicals when he engineered the whole scheme, and he'd hire every big name psychologist to come in and testify that personal responsibility is a myth. These days, Jameson would probably win that too."

"Jesus." But it fit. The inexorable conclusion of the Prozac generation: the will was not free. Either Jameson's hands were clean, or they were robotic tools programmed by brain chemicals. Albert drank, his hand trembling around the handle of the mug. He slammed the mug to the table, and eyed the green and white stained glass of the doors leading to the foyer. Could a robot fling the mug through the window? He shut his eyes and hung his head for a moment. "So what happened?"

"The assistant DA went to her boss, and came back to tell us they wouldn't prosecute. Wang flew to Singapore this morning and is never coming back."

"And Jameson's walking around with millions, courtesy of his dead wife." Poor little rich girl? How was that again? Albert looked at the tabletop, and raised a hand to mask his face.

Maria sucked up the last of her daiquiri. She frowned, then rested her hand on his. "Albert, I, I feel like a fool and I know it, but do you have plans for tonight? I could take a pizza home for us and Eddie, then get him into bed by nine."

"Maria—"

"I'm not talking about something long-term. I know it wouldn't work. Just tonight."

"I...." Why hesitate? So she had belly fat and a son who'd wonder about the noises coming from behind the wall. At his age and erratic position on the middle-class treadmill, a meaningless hookup with a woman like Maria was about the best Albert could get. Better than going home alone to down a six-pack and watch Super Bowl XXXII on ESPN Classic.

But not as good as connecting with someone, anyone, on a level more affirming than a five-minute slap of bodies. Even if they were puppets of brain chemicals, they could both act as if they had agency.

Albert's face firmed and his voice deepened. "Take home the pizza for us and your son. I'm not looking for emotionless sex. After Eddie goes to bed, we'll talk like two people with free will."

STRIKE PRICES

Strike price: The price at which a stock or commodity contract may be bought (upon exercise of a call option) or sold (upon exercise of a put option).

One Monday morning in January, Amer walked across the lawn from his house to his office. The sounds of south Florida's non-winter drifted to him from elsewhere in the gated community of acreage home sites. The distant buzz of mowers and edgers. The thwock of tennis balls from his neighbor's backyard court, hidden by an eight-foot vine-covered iron fence. The plash of an alligator slinking into the canal behind Amer's property.

His office had reinforced concrete walls two stories high, and a metal roof pressed and painted to look like red Spanish tiles. On a slab outside, the air conditioner condenser kicked into life as Amer approached.

At the door, he pressed his thumb to the fingerprint reader and exposed his retina to the scanner. Not even his wife or daughter could enter his office without him. With thuds and whirs, the door released its magnets and locks. Amer went inside.

After five minutes spent checking his office for signs of overnight intrusion, he settled into his upstairs desk chair. With the press of a button, he opened the curtains over the jalousie window. The window's slats striped the view of the canal and the boathouses and mansions beyond it. More biometrics and a twenty-character password later, the bank of computer monitors woke up.

A quick check of the markets, then Amer got to work on his current project. A shortage in electricity deliveries to the western terminus of the trans-Atlantic superconducting cable would drive up electricity prices. He already owned a sizable long position in March futures contracts, as well as call options at popular strike prices on those same contracts. He could buy more, but every additional purchase could clue others in to his strategy.

He massaged his forehead with long fingers. A shortage in photovoltaic electricity from Africa might boost the stock prices of alternative energy providers. Lockheed Martin, FusorX.... a boost for FusorX could increase demand for boron... how many boron futures contracts could he buy unnoticed—?

The videophone app popped up an incoming call notification. The field team?

He relaxed. Iasmine. His daughter. He opened the call.

The way her sweatshirt's hood bunched at her neck made her face like a flower opening from a gray bud. Her wide eyes, her unblemished skin, her oval face—she must know her beauty, but she dressed modestly and spoke of boys rarely, and only as distractions to her studies. She never pried about how he made his living and always treated Amer with proper respect.

Thank God. If she knew how little Amer could refuse her, she would ask for the moon, and he would neglect all else to acquire deed to it.

Despite his thoughts, he put on a paternal front. "Daughter, shouldn't you be in class?"

"I have a few minutes before I need to go."

"It must be cold there. Are you dressed warmly enough? Where are your hat and gloves?"

"By the door. Don't worry, father, I'll put them on when I leave." She took a breath. "While I have a few minutes, I called to ask you something."

Amer shook his head. "I will not raise your allowance—"

"Father, no, it's, spring break is coming in less than two months, and I'd like to take a trip this year."

"You don't want to come home?"

"It's not a party trip, father. Honestly. I've seen too many girls, and even some boys, come back the worse for spring break. I'd rather stay in my dorm than do that. No, it's a service trip. Brighton University Students for World Peace. They're going to central Asia to deliver refurbished phones and tablets to the Uyghurstan refugees." She widened her eyes and an icy part of him melted. "I want to go."

"Central Asia." Amer leaned back in his chair. "You think because there's no beach there won't be any partying?"

Her expression crinkled. "Father, please believe me, that's not why I want to go. There's no way to party there. The host agency requires RFID chips in every bottle of alcohol and insists male-female married couples from the faculty go along as chaperones."

Amer's mouth scrunched. "Even if that's so, I've told you, humanitarian aid doesn't work. It all goes to the warlords and corrupt bureaucrats, instead of the people it's supposed to help. Even if it got through to the intended people, it would only fuel the fire of the ongoing conflict. If you want peace, you have to let the wars burn themselves out."

"Father, I know you've said that, and I'm sure that's how it was when you were in college, but things are different now." Iasmine's face showed she was too immature to doubt the words she parroted. "We have social media, streaming video, and big data. This time, we can change the world. Please, father?"

"You're being naïve." Amer spoke softly. He'd already given in. The only remaining question was how much face could he save. "To allow you to go, I need to know which faculty members will chaperone, and I must talk to them before I can approve."

Iasmine smiled. "Father, thank you. That's very fair. I'll send you their contact info. And I won't ask for a penny. I'll buy my own ticket—"

"A coach ticket? You want to ride with your knees in your chest for fifteen hours? I have unused jetshare credits, you can—"

"A private jet?" Iasmine looked at him as if he wanted to repeal abolition. "To a refugee camp? I can't."

"It's a jetshare, not a private jet. And not you alone. It should fit the whole club."

"Father!"

Her tone dissuaded him. "A first class ticket, then."

"While my friends ride in coach? I don't want them thinking I'm a snooty rich girl."

"Your friends' fathers are all almost as wealthy as I." Amer said. He slapped his hand on his desk and she started. "If you want to fly coach, fine. But I will buy your ticket." Memories of prior projects stirred in the upper reaches of his subconscious. "On an airline of my choice. I insist."

"Father, thank you, but that's too generous." Iasmine tried to look serious,

Amer read from her face, but he could only see his daughter's youth as she went on. "I want to pay my own way."

"You can pay your own way after you are married. Send me those chaperone names. All this talk means nothing if I cannot approve you traveling with them."

She looked respectful. "Yes, father."

Within ten minutes of the call's end, Amer received her text message. He imagined her pulling down her scarf to dictate the message, exposing her nose and mouth to the bitter cold of a dead-brown winter campus. The lush Florida landscape outside the windows seemed unnatural in comparison. Amer wished his daughter were still a child, playing all winter in a sundress on the lawn.

He set the wistfulness aside. The world punished sentiment. He contacted a private investigator to dig into the backgrounds and personal lives of the chaperones, then returned to project planning.

A few minutes later, with boron volume and open interest data from the Chicago, London, and Shanghai exchanges filling his monitors, the videophone app popped up another notification. Iasmine again?

His heart slowed and slammed. Not a field team. Not Iasmine. The notification showed a code name which Amer swiftly transcribed in his mind. Heartstone, the CEO of TransAtlantic Airlines.

Amer tapped out commands. The blinds closed. In the lower left corner of his monitor array, a window opened to show a shifting, distorted animation. The animation made him think of ransom notes in old crime shows, with messages made from words and letters cut from magazines. Instead of words, the window showed an ever-changing composite face, its features copied from image searches. Green eyes, blond hair, an old drunk's blotched nose, thick African lips.

Amer turned his head and lifted his mouth's corners. In the window, the composite face showed sidelong a woman's blue eyes, a narrow nose with hidden nostrils, a half-smile on lips as narrow as a Finn's.

The window showed him the same image the other party on the videophone call would see.

Another window opened to the side of the composite face. Amer cleared his throat and multicolored lines jumped. An audio spectrum analyzer. He spoke a few test words, then repeated them. Different pattern each time. The voice disguiser worked properly.

A few more keystrokes, and Heartstone's image filled one of the monitors. Surprisingly, the workaholic from Brooklyn wore a plaid shirt, and a stone fireplace with a stuffed fish on the mantle formed the backdrop. A gray day shadowed the horizontal creases in Heartstone's forehead and bald scalp.

"Are the fish biting, Mr. Heartstone?"

Heartstone's words burst out of clamped lips. "You think I'm freezing my ass off wading for trout? I had to make up a cover story of a strategic retreat and waste an entire goddamn weekend out here just to call you. What the hell are you doing to me?"

Amer sat straighter, spoke softly. "I don't know what you mean."

His tone appeared to communicate the desired ominous quiet. Heartstone's eyebrows jerked upward. His voice sounded plaintive. "I've given you everything you asked for. Every month, regular as clockwork, right? Consulting fees, vendor invoices, it adds up to a million. To the penny. You're getting our deposits, right?"

"Yes." TransAtlantic Airlines was one of a dozen large corporations who paid Amer to keep their businesses safe.

Impotent anger, like an old gasoline engine revving in neutral, spiked in Heartstone's features, almost too quickly to see. "So, why?"

"What do you think I have done?"

"TransAtlantic has some employees check trading activity on our stock and options," Heartstone said. "We have to, everyone else does, it would look suspicious if I canceled—"

"One must keep up appearances," Amer said.

"Last week they found about five million dollars worth of hostile activity. Naked shorts. An increase in open interest with a corresponding drop in asking prices for out-of-the-money calls with June expirations. A bid up on out-of-the-money June puts at strike prices of 50, 52.5, and 55."

From decades in his line of work, Amer understood the jargon. Someone had bet that TransAtlantic's stock price would fall before June. Short sales of the stock, and options to sell short more of the stock, would become profitable. That someone wanted to make more money by writing options to buy TransAtlantic's stock above the current price. Not to keep, but to sell to others in the expectation they would expire worthless: exchange-traded pigs in a poke.

On one of his monitors, Amer opened TransAtlantic's share price and options charts. The stock had traded quietly for months, with a current price of about 65. The put options referred to by Heartstone had current prices from 1.50 to 3.00.

If TransAtlantic's share price dropped into the upper forties before June, the naked shorts, purchased on margin, would turn a 30% profit. The real money would be made on the put options: profits in the range of 100%, 200%, not including the time value the puts would gain if the price dropped earlier than June.

Amer had made comparable profits many times over the years.

"And my people dug into who did this to us," Heartstone said. "Not individuals, not established hedge funds. Shell companies out of the Caymans, the Netherlands Antilles, the Persian Gulf. Different company names, but the same sorts of countries where we send your million dollars a month. So I thought of you."

"It is not me."

Heartstone ducked his gaze from his camera. He raised a shaking fist, then thudded it against his thigh. "Why did I make this goddam call you're not going to shoot straight—"

"To the contrary," Amer said. "I will be completely truthful. We have an agreement which benefits us both. If I broke that agreement for a short-term gain, my reputation would suffer. You would never trust me again. You would urge your counterparts at other large companies to never trust me either. Whatever you think of my business model, you cannot fault my logic."

"I can't. Dammit." Heartstone's lips clamped together for a moment. "How tight is your ship?"

"You think one of my subordinates has done this without my knowledge?" Impossible. Amer's brother, his cousins, his nephews, their talents served best in the field. They knew their limitations regarding the financial markets. And they knew without family loyalty, the world would crush them one by one. "I assure you, they have not."

Heartstone lowered his head to his hand. "Then who?"

"It is very easy to form a legal entity in those countries you mentioned. It could be done through gray and dark networking from anywhere on Earth. Even from an office at TransAtlantic's headquarters."

Heartstone's face loomed into the videophone window. "You know something? One of my own insiders is out to ream me?"

"I am ignorant of the internal politics at your company. However, it is plausible someone is aware of news that, once released, will depress your stock price."

"No. My ship's as tight as yours. No one's hiding a time bomb like that from me. They know better."

Amer shrugged. "If you say so." Heartstone deluded himself. No blood bound his subordinates to him; only money, a far weaker force. A big enough company grew tumors, malignant bodies where executives like oncogenes shirked their duty to the body and sought only their own aggrandizement, regardless of the wider cost.

Such would not befall Amer. If a tumor ever arose, he would nip it before it became malignant.

"If that's all, Mr. Heartstone?"

A pensive look on his face, Heartstone nodded. Amer hung up.

The next weeks passed quietly. Amer entered a few more positions: long boron futures, boron mining exchange-traded bull funds, a few plays in African stocks. Ten million dollars slid around the world, a few keystrokes at a time.

One Thursday morning in February, atypically for his usual workflow, he turned one of his monitors over to a televised news stream. A camera, apparently helicopter-mounted, zoomed in on an electrical station sited in desert on the shore of a choppy gray sea. Fires crackled in the station. A small rubble pile lay at the sea's edge. Crumpled swarthy men wearing deep blue uniforms lay around the site, accented by red splotches on the rocky soil.

Something filled the camera view. It took a few seconds for the camera to autofocus on it. A small meter, held in a white man's weathered hand. The meter's digital display showed a virtual needle wobbling back and forth between a yellow zone and a red.

"We have to move the helicopter back from the site." A voice, white South African by accent, presumably belonging to the man holding the meter. "As you can see from the Geiger counter, we're picking up unsafe radiation levels. This clearly confirms the rebel claims posted to the internet, that they detonated a dirty bomb on the site."

The South African lowered the meter. The helicopter banked. The camera autofocused on a miles-long array of purplish-black solar panels. Early afternoon sunlight filled part of the array with a glare. "Between the radioactivity release and the damage to the eastern terminus of the trans-Atlantic superconducting cable, the United States won't get solar electricity from Mauritania for weeks, maybe months."

Satisfaction lifted the corners of Amer's mouth. He turned his attention to the markets. The heatmaps showing price action in electricity futures boiled with fluorescent green. High volume, with every transaction at a higher price than the last. Turning to boron futures and boron mining stocks, green simmered in their heatmaps. Prices climbed in all the instruments in which he'd painstakingly added positions over the prior months. News stories headlined the obvious, *Electricity Futures Rise on Terrorist Attack on Superconducting Cable.*

Time to cash in.

Amer started selling his futures contracts and call options. In all the markets, today's volume would be very high, giving him leeway to exit his positions in much larger chunks than he had entered. He doubled his investment that morning.

With a fraction of his attention, he listened to the newscast. The National Front for the Liberation of South Mauritania claimed responsibility for the attack. Talking heads and suited experts filled long minutes discussing the rebels. Amer soon realized none of them had any clue about Mauritania or its internal conflicts.

Not that Amer did, either. Some ethnic grievance dressed up in politically correct language of freedom, self-determination, civil liberties, human rights. No matter. The rebels had served their purpose and could now be jettisoned. A people either oppresses or is oppressed. All that ever changed was who wielded the whip and who felt its bite. Such was the way of the world. The fraction of his attention devoted to the news grew even smaller.

An expert said, "The sophistication of the attack suggests foreigners must have been involved."

Amer started. The reporter's next words to the expert came to Amer as if through a fog. "You're saying Africans are incapable of building and deploying a dirty bomb?"

The expert looked alarmed for a moment. "No, no, nothing like that, Africans are as capable of terrorism as anyone else, though clearly they would only be driven to terrorism by intractable and unjust opposition by the Western world...."

Amer let out a long breath. With relaxed shoulders, he turned back to the markets, to sell more futures contracts and newly in-the-money call options.

The morning hummed along, with only one interruption, around noon. An email from the field team, posing as freelance soccer scouts. *We're in the Sahrawi Republic now. Found some promising talent across the border in Mauritania. No other scouts in the area. Full details when we get back.*

Mission successful, and the field team had gone unnoticed by the Mauritanian authorities. Good. He would debrief them after they returned to Florida. And right away, this time. Not another two-week delay in which their knowledge would leak out of their minds and Amer would forget the questions he wanted to ask. A blunder, that previous debriefing had been. No harm had come, though. They had a stable and secure business model that remained unseen by law enforcement around the world.

Amer shook his head to clear his train of thought. He had a few days before the field team would arrive. Now—after lunch, rather. He hadn't gone out for lunch in a week—he would return his attention to the markets and take even more profits.

One Friday morning in the middle of March, Amer sat in his office. After reviewing the technical specs of a desalinization plant on the Mexican coast one-hundred-eighty miles south-southwest of Phoenix, and buying shares of California- and Texas-based desalinization utilities and freight haulers, he took a break to skim a catalog of carbon nanotube golf clubs. A sunny day outside and the passing of someone's boat down the canal made him want to golf more—

His office's doorbell rang. The camera feed showed his wife, her eyes sunken.

Amer opened the intercom. "In here is where I earn the money that supports are family. You know you are not to enter—"

"Please come to the house." She spoke quietly.

What did she overreact at? Amer frowned, then minimized the golf catalog and locked his computer. Moments later he exited his office.

His wife said nothing. She shuffled toward the house. He quickened his steps, but she reached for his hand. "Walk with me. Please, Amer."

"What has happened?"

She opened her mouth. No words came. Her eyes glistened with moisture. She shuffled along, her grip tight.

In the enclosed porch, the audio track of a newscast came from the living room. "Truly a terrible scene. Wreckage strewn for miles. I can't imagine any survivors."

A chill feeling washed through Amer. His wife released her grip. He walked into the living room as icy hands of fear clutched at his legs.

The ultra-high-def filled half the far wall. So large was the screen, he could easily read, above images of a dusty plain interspersed with torn fragments of metal, the headline.

TransAtlantic Crash in Central Asia.

The camera feed from the crash site cut out, replaced with an anchorman in the studio. "For those of you just joining us, a TransAtlantic airlines flight from

Almaty to Boston crashed shortly after takeoff. Preliminary reports indicate there were no survivors."

The anchorman went on. "The passengers included a group of Brighton University students returning from a humanitarian spring break trip...."

Amer heard nothing more for a time. Neither the anchorman nor his wife's whimpers. He imagined Iasmine's last moments. God willing she had passed out before the plane struck the ground.

"A number of witnesses report three missiles were fired at the airplane. At least one hit. A group calling itself the National Front for the Liberation of East Turkestan has claimed responsibility."

He misspoke, South Mauritania—my god—

The anchorman continued. "In its statement, the NFLET says it targeted this flight because of the Brighton University group on board. 'Their humanitarian purpose was a fig leaf for their evil origins. These people were the children of the bloated plutocrats who for centuries have sucked the lifeblood out of the developing world. Now their parents know the pain their monopolist policies have inflicted on us.' "

Amer struggled to lift his gaze to the crawl at the bottom of the screen. Stock prices scrolled by.

TransAtlantic's ticker symbol appeared, followed by a red, downward-pointing arrow, and numbers. *47.52. -17.35. -26.7%.*

Ted Williams Eyes

Cooper jogged out of the Astros clubhouse and up the dugout steps toward the batting cage. Echoing around nearly-empty TeXolar Power Park, cameras whirred and reporters shouted questions. Magazines, websites, and TV from around the world, all here to see him take batting practice before the final game of the season.

Back in the stands, a hundred fans in team colors cheered. Cooper lifted his batting helmet. Just like the reporters, they didn't come to find out if Astros would finish four games out of playoff contention, or five. They didn't even come to see if tonight's opponent, the in-state rival Rangers, would make the wild card with a win. They came to see Cooper make history.

No matter what happened tonight, Cooper would have the highest single season batting average since Gwynn way back in '94. With a couple of hits, he would be the first ballplayer in almost a century to reach—

"Four-oh-oh! Four-oh-oh!" Twelve rows back, a pudgy fan in a retro '70s-style Astros jersey, with a flat-brimmed cap and a dime-sized beard patch between his mouth and chin, chanted. Others joined in.

Playfully, Cooper shook his head, then put on his helmet and went to the warm-up circle. He slid donut weights onto his bat handle.

A reporter in the front row called out, "Even if you miss .400, you've gained a hundred points in batting average over last season! Is it true performance-enhancing drugs explain it?"

Cooper checked his warm-up swing and peered at the reporter. Bob Jackson, from purebaseball.com. Jackson needed to trim the hair in his nose and do a better job concealing the pimples on his neck. "You know how many times I've peed in a cup this year." He looked at the other clustered reporters. "Anyone have a real question?"

A reporter from Japan asked, "How else can you explain your great improvement in all offensive statistics?"

Despite his long-sleeved uniform and the slice of blue, cloud-puffed Texas sky through the open roof, Cooper shivered. Could anyone have found out? His childhood friend, Derek Liu, now a biotech entrepreneur in Singapore, had paid all of his travel expenses to Derek's new CRISPR/Cas9 clinic. He'd checked into the hotel under an assumed name....

He rested the bat across his shoulders. No one would ever know. "I'm seeing the ball better. That's all." He lowered the bat and tapped the handle on the ground. The donut weights clattered to the grass. "Time for me to get to work."

Cooper strode to the batting cage, waggling his bat. Among the group waiting their turns stood the team's three next best batters. Odysseus Skelton, the stocky first baseman, rolling his lips while undoing and redoing the hook-and-loop fasteners on his batting gloves. Chalo Dominguez, the rookie left fielder, his hand on the crucifix hanging around his neck and his eyes squeezed in prayer. For a 22-year-old, Dominguez had a broad tracery of crow's-feet at the corners of his eyes. Jordan Himmelblau, the shortstop, facial muscles bunched and jaw working like a piston on his chewing gum.

Sometimes, your teammates became friends. Others, they were just guys you worked with.

Himmelblau spoke. "Here comes Mr. Ted Williams eyes."

The Hall of Famer, last man to bat .400, but—"What about his eyes?" Cooper asked.

"Legend has it Williams had 20/3 vision. Talk about seeing the ball better."

Cooper shivered again. Did Himmelblau somehow know?

No. He wanted to know his secret, of course, no less than the reporters. But the reporters just wanted click bait. His teammates wanted the magic to rub off on them so they too could become rich free agents after their contracts expired.

Cooper returned a flat stare. Only one player could become baseball's first half-billion dollar man.

"Next group, your turn," the BP coach called. "Coop, get in here."

Cooper gave Himmelblau, Skelton, and Dominguez one last look. "Watch and learn, boys."

Inside the cage, he stopped outside the right-handed batter's box and raised his bat in front of his eyes. Fine details in the wood grain and minute scorched curlicues in the manufacturer's brand seemingly jumped to his eye. Used to it now, but the first time he'd studied a bat after Derek Liu's gene therapy, newly-visible details had stunned him.

He shut his eyes, drew in a breath. An early summer day came to him, cloudless sky, field greened by dozens of child-league fathers. Eight years old, coming up to bat against a kid from the opposing team for the first time.

The other boy put the ball over the middle of the plate. A smooth swing. The ping of the ball against the aluminum bat. The white dot shrinking as the ball flew up and away. His lips parted, his gaze rapt, his heart soaring with the ball.

He'd liked baseball before then. From that moment, he'd loved it.

Cooper opened his eyes and stepped into the batter's box.

The coach swiped and tapped his phone. The pitching machine light glowed green, ready to fling balls in the style of Huerta, tonight's opposing starting pitcher.

The machine whipped forward its arm and released the ball. It looked as big as a full moon. Cooper read the seams pulsing across the visible face as if he watched slow motion video. He swung, arms whipping the bat head through the zone.

The ball sliced to right-center, higher than a second baseman could catch, low enough to fall in front of the outfielders.

Slider, thigh-high, outer half. He nodded to himself, then dug in his cleats for the next pitch.

A different pulse of seams, a different trajectory leaving the mechanical hand. He swung.

Line drive. The ball clattered against the pitching screen. The coach jumped, then nodded and gave a thumbs-up. "Do that in the game and he won't try his curve."

Cooper set his feet, cocked his bat. Dust motes drifted in air near the machine's arm. "Ready."

Fastballs, cutters, changeups, curves, sliders. He read them all an instant after the machine released them. He pulled some, went the opposite way on others, lining most for what would be singles or doubles. He sent one ball to Tal's hill, the flagpole mound inside the fence in dead center, another into the boxes behind the short fence in left field.

He nodded to himself. He'd found his groove. "I'm ready to play, coach."

*　　*　　*

In the locker room, every player prepped for the game in his own way. Cooper imbibed sports drink. Dominguez listened to bachata music loudly leaking from his earbuds. Ode Skelton played dominoes with two guys from the bullpen.

Himmelblau unrolled his tablet and read baseball news. He quickly swiped past stories about Cooper's chase of .400, then lingered over an article, raking his fingers through his wiry hair as he read. "Huh."

Cooper capped his bottle of sports drink. "Don't leave us hanging."

"A local sabermetrics blogger speculating about next year. He says if you stay at your new level, and three other guys on the team matched your same spike in offensive statistics, we'd win a hundred games."

Cooper's eyes widened. A hundred wins. Five teams a decade reached that mark. Division champions for sure, probable home-field advantage through the league playoffs. The best chance of any team of winning the World Series.

He leaned back in his chair and folded his arms. Year after next, he could get as good a chance of winning the World Series as a free agent signed with a perennial power, like St. Louis or Kansas City. He opened his mouth, but Skelton spoke before he could.

"Man, that stathead stuff is flim-flam."

Himmelblau lightly smacked his palm against his high forehead. "I keep telling you, Ode, advanced statistics have value. Coop's OPS has gone up 343 points this year."

"What's that OSP business again?"

"OPS." Himmelblau scowled. "On base percentage plus slugging percentage. The sabermetricians have correlations between OPS and runs created, and from runs created to the Pythagorean win projection. Our Pythagorean win projection this year is spot on—"

Ode Skelton shook his head. "Come on, man, formulas don't play the game. We do. Ain't that right, Cha-lllooowww?"

Dominguez blinked a few times. "I just want to play. Give 110%. Every game."

"You see?" Skelton said to Himmelblau. "You with me too, Coop?"

He shrugged. "Most GMs these days pay attention to the statheads." Cooper stood, sports drink bulging his bladder. "Time to hit the head."

After taking a leak, Cooper went to the sinks under the broad, paneled mirror. He washed his hands by feel. His gaze landed on his reflection's crow's-feet and wisps of graying hair. Even a long career would end in another dozen years.

Would you rather have half a billion dollars, or a World Series ring?

He shook his head, flicked water off his fingertips. His secret trip to Derek Liu's gene therapy lab meant he would get both.

From the main part of the locker room came manager Gray Wade's hand claps. "Saddle up, men! Time to win a ball game!"

A minute later, the team filed out of the clubhouse. Music from the stadium PA and the noise of thirty thousand spectators funneled down. Amazingly large crowd for a home team already eliminated from playoff contention.

Cooper jogged up the dugout steps. A cheer erupted from the crowd, echoing from the upper decks and the closed parts of the retractable roof. The chant began. "Four-oh-oh! Four-oh-oh!"

He lifted his cap. Half a billion dollars and a World Series ring? He was on track for both.

For his first plate appearance, Cooper came up with bases empty and two outs in the bottom of the first. The colossal video screen behind center showed his picture and, in giant alphanumerics, *AB 591. H 236. BA .399.* The crowd shouted and clapped. Cooper stepped into the box like he walked on air.

The opposing pitcher, Huerta, pulled his cap low over his eyes and peered at the catcher's signals. He nodded, then started his windup.

The ball left Huerta's glove. Cooper read it instantly, kept his bat over his shoulder. Curveball, going low.

The pitch skipped off the dirt in front of the plate, then into the catcher's glove. Ball one.

Cooper grinned. "All he's got tonight?"

"He's got enough," the catcher replied, "to keep you below .400."

Huerta looked for the next signal. Nod, windup. A fastball low and heading outside. Cooper's bat stayed on his shoulder.

"Stee-rike!" the umpire called.

Cooper looked back. The umpire's lowered eyebrows dared him to argue. Cooper blew out a breath. The fine detail of the batmaker's label caught his gaze for a moment, returned part of him to that little league field decades ago.

Huerta's next pitches nibbled the edges of the umpire's generous strike zone. The count reached 2-2. A fastball left the pitcher's hand on a trajectory low and inside.

Cooper swung. The ball skipped hard off the infield grass and dirt, on a line to thread the needle between the shortstop and third baseman. The crowd shouted with excitement. A hard grounder dribbling into the outfield would give him that one more hit.

He raced toward first base. The crowd noise suddenly gained a nervous edge. Cooper stretched his leg, his foot descending, inches from the bag—

The ball smacked into the first baseman's glove. Cooper's foot struck the base. He ran through and turned his head, face tight, watching the first base umpire. *Come on, they haven't replaced you with robots yet, make this your one blown call all season.*

The first base umpire raised his right fist.

Cooper walked back to the dugout, head turned to the video screen for the replay. The shortstop got a great jump on the ball, extended his glove at the last moment, and quickly planted his foot to make a perfect throw.

Nothing you can do. Cooper trotted down the dugout steps.

His second plate appearance came in the fourth. Nobody on, one out. Direct rays of the setting sun partially washed out the video display, but the key numbers remained readable. *AB 592. H 236. BA .399.*

Cooper took the first pitch, a four-seamer outside, and soon worked the count to 3-1.

Huerta looked at the catcher's signs, and his black eyebrows crinkled. The expression faded and he came set.

Cooper guessed at the next pitch even before it left Huerta's palm. Change-up. Cooper shifted his weight into his swing.

The crack of the bat rang for a moment, then the crowd roared. Cooper watched as he ran into foul territory to round first. High enough, hard enough, it could clear the wall in left-center. On the balcony jutting over the wall, fans holding half-full cups of beer next to the solar-powered home run tally board reached out one-handed.

The center fielder's cleats dug dirt from the warning track. Directly under the balcony, he leaped, right arm mashing the wall. His glove plucked the ball from the air inches above and beyond the bright yellow stripe.

Thirty thousand voices groaned. Cooper jogged back to the dugout.

His third plate appearance came in the sixth inning, Himmelblau on first, two out, score tied 0-0. The scoreboard blazed *AB 593. H 236. BA .398.*

Lips pressed together, Huerta shook off signs throughout. He stayed away from his curve, throwing his other pitches—slider, two-seam fastball, Vulcan changeup. 3-2 count.

Huerta threw a slider. Cooper swung. A line drive, slicing well above the second baseman's reach. The ball landed deep in the right-center gap and motored toward the wall. The crowd sounded like a rock concert or an airplane runway.

The two nearest outfielders sprinted after the ball. Cooper sprinted too. Nearing second, he looked ahead to the third-base coach. Coach waved him through, then made the stop sign.

Cooper slid into third, well ahead of the relayed throw. He called time and brushed dirt off his knee, looking at the team's dugout.

At home, players high-fived Himmelblau. He returned the gesture, then glanced toward Cooper. A crisp nod, then he trotted to the dugout steps.

The Astros led 1-0. Cooper on third. Two out, but time for more. He shouted toward the plate. "Come on, Ode!"

Skelton, a left-handed batter, spat tobacco juice and stepped in. He held his bat straight up, rocking the barrel back and forth more forcefully than usual. With narrow eyes he watched the pitcher.

Don't swing for the fences, Ode. A single to the outfield scores the run.

Huerta threw a fastball, low and away. Ode lifted his right foot but held back his bat.

"Steee-rike," called the umpire. Some fans booed. Ode gave the umpire a mean look, then shook his head and stepped back in for the next pitch.

Next pitch, a changeup. *Be patient—*

Ode swung too early. The ball chopped foul past the home dugout. The ballboy tossed it to a small child on the fourth row.

Now an 0-2 count. Huerta smirked. The next pitch, a curveball. Cooper's heart hung, ready to drop with the breaking ball. Ode swung, waist high. The pitch crossed the plate at his knees.

"Steee-rike three. You're out!"

Ode flipped his bat end-over-end to the grass as he trudged back to the dugout.

The seventh and eighth innings went quickly, with the Astros going three-up-three-down in both frames. The crowd grew restless. A fan in the front row behind the dugout told someone that Cooper's triple had only gotten him back to .399. Cooper would come up second in the bottom of the ninth—if the Astros batted.

Top of the ninth, the Astros still led 1-0.

The Astros' closer stalked around the mound as the PA blared *Flight of the Valkyries*. He took the mound, his brows lowered, the image of focus on getting the save regardless of Cooper's pursuit of .400. But the closer's first pitches missed the plate and he gave up a leadoff single to a speedy runner. A pickoff throw went wide and the runner slid into second.

Tying run in scoring position, a right-handed pull hitter at bat, the second baseman shifted to join Cooper and Himmelblau on the third-base side of the infield. Cooper took position with his right foot almost touching the foul line.

If the batter lines one you can't handle, tie game and you get one more chance in the bottom of the ninth.

Cooper blinked. He slammed his right hand into his glove and watched the batter.

The batter fouled the first pitch back off the screen, then took the second low and in. Third pitch, fastball on the inside half of the plate. Swing, crack.

Cooper's feet shifted to his left. His glove hand rose. He looked back the runner on second, then rifled a one-hop throw to Skelton at first. One out.

He paced across the dirt to his usual fielding spot. On his way, he nodded to himself. He'd done the right thing without thinking, from habit born on that distant sunny field of his youth.

Warmth filled his chest. Your line in the box score didn't matter. Winning a ball game mattered.

The next batter came up. He fouled off four pitches before the closer left a curveball hanging. Well hit to left. Cooper's shoulders sagged as the ball sailed over his head. It landed in the seats, five rows back and five feet inside the foul pole.

The Astros now trailed 2-1. He would get that one more chance.

To start the bottom of the ninth, a pitch struck Himmelblau in the thigh. The closer, Ryerson, had a nasty curve and slider, when in the groove. The scoreboard blazed *AB 594. H 237. BA .399.* The crowd came to its feet, chanting "Four-oh-oh! Four-oh-oh!"

Energy jittered into Cooper's arms and legs. He raised his bat and that memory from his childhood returned, grounding the energy. Calm, focused, he stepped in.

Ryerson came set and Cooper decided to take the first pitch. The ball left the pitcher's hand. A slider, low and outside, but it would probably catch the corner of the umpire's generous strike zone.

"Ball."

The catcher tossed the ball back to the pitcher, then looked over his shoulder. "Low or outside?" he asked the umpire.

"Outside," the umpire replied in a firm tone.

Cooper smiled to himself. This plate appearance just got easier.

Next pitch, curveball, breaking too hard. It hit the dirt in front of the plate and skipped under the catcher's glove. Cooper jumped back and waved Himmelblau forward. The ball rolled to the backstop, catcher chasing it. Himmelblau slid headfirst into second. The catcher didn't even throw.

2-0 count, and no chance of hitting into a double play. A base hit would score the tying run.

The next pitch. Another curveball, this one would barely break. Cooper shifted his weight and lashed out with his hands.

It broke even less than Cooper expected. He caught it low and it sliced foul, landing in the second deck behind the home dugout. The crowd noise lulled, then picked back up as Ryerson readied his next pitch.

Fastball, sailing high. Cooper leaned back. The catcher rose from his crouch and extended his mitt. The pitch smacked leather. The catcher tossed the ball back to Ryerson, then made a settle-down gesture with his hands.

3-1. Thousands of voices took up the chant. "Four-oh-oh! Four-oh-oh!"

If Ryerson missed the zone again, foul it off or take ball four?

Cooper readied the bat and turned his augmented eyes to the pitcher. The wrist snap, the roll off the fingers, the spinning seams, a slider, inside, he could foul it off—

The bat stayed over Cooper's shoulder. "Ball four!"

Boos drizzled down on Ryerson from the first fans to realize the walk would not get Cooper back up to .400. The boos rained down as Cooper dropped the bat and jogged to first base. Then the boos broke up, giving way to applause and cheers. A new chant sprung up. "MVP! MVP!"

Cooper stopped at first and doffed his batting helmet to the crowd. He turned, taking in the fans all around the park. A glow filled his chest.

Then his gaze met Himmelblau's. His teammate gave one curt nod.

The glow remained. Cooper nodded back.

Nearby, the first base umpire stepped back to position. Still three outs left in the game. Cooper reseated his helmet, stuffed his batting gloves into his back pocket, and looked to the plate. "Come on, Ode!"

Skelton squirted tobacco juice from his mouth and stepped into the box. He worked the barrel of the bat forward and back, as usual, but from the fraction of his face visible to Cooper, Skelton seemed more relaxed than he had in the sixth.

Ode took a pitch outside, dribbled foul a strike on his hands. 1-1. Next, Ryerson flung a fastball on a chest-high trajectory.

Cooper sucked in a breath. Skelton's arms tensed, but he didn't swing. "Ball!" called the umpire.

The catcher tossed the ball back to Ryerson. 2-1. Ryerson stepped to the rubber, came set. The pitch. A slider, running in, not far enough.

Skelton lined the ball to right-center. Cheers thundered from the crowd. Cooper ran the instant he saw the ball would hit the ground. The third base coach waved him all the way through.

Cooper's foot jabbed third and he headed home. He looked over his shoulder. On the warning track, the right fielder bent down for the ball.

A grin split Cooper's mouth. Himmelblau stood behind home plate, hands high, waving him in standing up. Near the on-deck circle, Dominguez lifted his bat into the air. In front of the plate, the catcher stood with face mask up and a dejected set to his shoulders. Cooper ran hard, as hard as that eight-year-old in his memory. Another glance toward right-center showed the ball arching slowly toward the cut-off man.

Cooper ran across the plate. Himmelblau wrapped an arm around him. Dominguez jumped in. Players and coaches streamed from the dugout and joined the pile. Skelton high-fived teammates and shouted, "That's what I'm talking 'bout!"

The crowd roared. Fireworks burst above the open roof. The scoreboard behind center showed graphics and numbers and a snorting 8-bit bull. Cooper could only make out the final score, 3-2.

Slowly, the cluster of coaches and players drifted toward the dugout. Fans on the front row chanted "MVP! MVP!"

Cooper lifted his batting helmet. Something deep in his mind clicked, and he extended his arms, taking in Skelton, Dominguez, Himmelblau, and the rest of the team.

The chant died away. The cheers mounted, echoing around the stadium, pouring out the open roof toward the city, flowing with the team down the dugout steps and the tunnel to the clubhouse.

* * *

An hour later, the clubhouse was nearly empty. Only four players remained, dressed in tailored suits, hair slick from showers, styling products, and Dominguez' black hair dye. Cooper stood in front of his locker, facing the others.

"Alright, we're alone," Skelton said. "What you got to say?"

Himmelblau nodded. "We're all curious."

"Yes, yes," added Dominguez.

Cooper took a deep breath. "I've been thinking about what Himmelblau said before the game." He twisted his upper body, pulled a tablet from the top shelf of his locker. From the end of the rolled-up tablet came the glow of the private, password-protected, encrypted website he'd already loaded.

Himmelblau's forehead creased. "You have a way for us each to gain three hundred points of OPS?"

"Yes." A grin tightened Cooper's cheeks. He unfurled the tablet and snapped it rigid. On the display, Dr. Derek Liu looked authoritative in lab coat and eyeglasses, under the caption *Singapore Clinic for Personal Improvement*.

Cooper said, "I'll show all three of you where to get Ted Williams eyes."

THE ULTIMATE WAGER

Under low, roiling clouds, the electric bus from New Madison crept down the streets of the alien city.

Near the front of the bus, holding onto a ceiling strap, Connor Little peered through the crowd. The Hspa Nki, seven feet tall with bluish-gray skin, walked on two backward legs. Thin glide membranes, translucent and veined, joined the two triple-jointed arms on each side. A light breeze rustled the dense patterns of beads, indicators of rank and role, tied to their tail quills. Their voices struck the bus like a downpour on a metal roof. From the din, Connor's comm implant could only extract the words *vacuum breathers*.

Never mind the planet's natives. Where were the explorers from Earth?

There had to be other humans nearby. A week ago, a ship had descended past the high plateau the human colonists called New Madison, toward this alien city in their planet's lowlands. An Exploration Consortium ship, it had to be. The descending ship must have seen the buildings, farms, and fabs of New Madison.

The crowd thickened. The bus lurched forward a few yards at a time.

No explorers from Earth showed amidst the Hspa Nki.

On an open field beyond a thinner part of the crowd, Hspa Nki threw flying discs made of some thin, pliable material regurgitated by one of the native bugs. The Hspa Nki were left-handed. Their backhand throws wobbled, but their forehand throws zipped and they plucked passes from the air.

Connor wavered on his feet. These Hspa Nki had failed to be picked for the aliens' ultimate flying disc team.

Explorers from Earth can't help you. You have to win this game on your own.

He rubbed his neck and shook out his free arm. The Hspa Nki had first seen a flying disc a week before, when they'd come up to the plateau to suddenly demand a retroactive land tax. Just because they had taken to throwing and catching the disc didn't mean they grasped ultimate's tactics—offensive stacks, defensive formations and marking, and more. The people of New Madison had played ultimate for thirty years, ever since *Bascom Hall*'s crash on this planet turned them from explorers to colonists.

A Hspa Nki drifted past the bus on spread glide membranes. Lucas, one of the New Madison all-stars, frowned. "Coach, if they can glide like that..."

Connor raised his voice to carry to all the players on the bus. "I insisted to Nednennik, the Hspa Nki's representative, that their players be forbidden from gliding to get open or catch a disc. Or catching with more than two hands. Nednennik agreed."

Lucas eased back in his seat, and the other players relaxed. Good, stay loose, ready to play.

Connor wished he could. Lose, and the New Madison colonists would be expelled from this planet; sent back to an Earth he and the other older colonists wouldn't recognize, and the younger ones, including all the players, had never known.

The bus' air conditioning labored as they approached a gap in a long, tall, knobby structure. Even after they went through the gap and parked in a cavernous garage, the air in the bus cloaked Connor like a steamy bathroom. Then they stepped out and the effect intensified. The air seemed almost chewy.

He inhaled. Chewy, but oxygen rich.

Outside the bus, a Hspa Nki lifted and spread its quills. Its haws blinked over its eyes.

Connor turned his palms up. "Honored host, I am Connor Little, son of...." He rattled off the names of his parents, still alive up on the New Madison plateau, and his grandparents, last seen before he left Earth as a teenager.

The Hspa Nki replied with a long list of ancestors, indicating low rank. "Honored guests, your fellows wait in the preparation chamber." It stretched all four arms toward a rounded doorway.

Connor's whole body quivered, like filings exposed to a magnet. Did the Hspa Nki mean—? "Fellows?"

"Yes." It held its arms in place. "They wait."

On unsteady feet, Connor led the team toward the rounded doorway. Lights inside pulled him closer, but part of him resisted. People from Earth, but why hadn't they come up the plateau to New Madison?

He went into the preparation chamber.

Flexible lighting panels, obviously human-made, clung to the regurgitated-brick ceiling. The panels illuminated two men.

"We've found our lost colleagues from the crash of *Bascom Hall*!" one said. He had thick black eyebrows curling down at the ends. Tall, with ropy limbs, he strode forward. Something about him seemed familiar. "I'm Vijay Rambard."

The room around Connor shrank away from his vision. Autumn evenings, the 3D in his parents' house on Earth. "I watched you when I was a kid. That championship series, against Denver, '72..." Connor's face warmed. A championship series Rambard's team lost.

A wince flickered over Rambard's face. "Always glad to meet a fan. But though I'm proud of my ultimate career, I've been a xenodiplomat with the Exploration Consortium for twenty years." He gestured at the other man. "This is Ernst Gonçalves. One of the Consortium's benefactors." A sour tone crept into his voice.

Benefactor? Some rich man salving his greedy conscience with donations to the Exploration Consortium. Connor's face tightened.

Gonçalves' head, neck, and shoulders flowed together, and his stomach lapped his belt. "You must tell me all about your colony," Gonçalves said around labored breaths. "Surviving a massive hyperjump malfunction, the loss of your ansible and emergency beacon, and a crash landing on an alien planet. Earth's audiences will clamor for your story."

"And you'll take fifteen percent?" Connor asked.

Gonçalves' face soured. "Mr. Little—"

"They aren't here to sell 3D rights." Rambard's tone sliced through the air. "Not everything is about making money."

Gonçalves peered at Rambard through droopy eyes. "I don't need you to tell me that."

Rambard rolled his eyes. "You amassed five billion dollars—"

To Connor, Gonçalves said, "We'll discuss your story later. We have much else to discuss now."

Connor's comm implant flashed a fifteen-minute warning across his vision. "And not much time." He turned to the players. "Change clothes and get ready.

Now!"

The players took their duffel bags to cubbies along the far wall. They changed into uniform shorts, jerseys, and cleats, and tossed bottles of sports drinks to one another.

"While the players ready themselves," Rambard said to Connor, "we'll tell you what we know or infer. As soon as our ship entered orbit, the Hspa Nki realized we had much more advanced technology than you were able to preserve from *Bascom Hall*'s wreckage."

Connor bristled. "We've done fine. A fusion reactor for power, a self-driving electric bus...." Obsolete toys compared to what Earth must have developed in the last thirty years. "Go on."

Gonçalves spoke, his words punctuated by heavy breaths. "The Hspa Nki only confirmed to us your colony existed after they imposed on you a tax you could not pay. But apparently they love to wager?"

"We're sure they never saw a flying disc, let alone an ultimate game, before they came up the plateau to New Madison and demanded all our technologies and almost all our production for the next decade."

"Their wager is a negotiating ploy," Gonçalves said. "They offered to waive your land tax if the Consortium paid them ten billion dollars."

Connor's mouth fell open. Finally he found words. "You didn't pay?"

Gonçalves' jowls shook with his head. "The Consortium cannot agree to so large an expenditure in a few days. We all wish it could."

Rambard chuffed out a breath. "Speak for yourself. We don't need to pay the Hspa Nki. Connor, your team will win this game. Because I'll be their coach."

Thick warm air flowed into Connor's lungs. Rambard might be a former star player, but—"I'm their coach."

"I played eight seasons in the North American Ultimate Flying Disc League. Decades later, I'm still in the top ten for many career stat categories."

Gonçalves cleared his throat. "In regular season games."

From under thick eyebrows, Rambard glowered sidelong at Gonçalves. "And I know firsthand how elevation impacts disc flight."

Connor's forehead furrowed. "Flight is flight, right?" Nearby, one of his players nodded.

"You don't leave your plateau, do you?"

Arms spread, Connor quickly said, "The Hspa Nki monitor anyone crossing the perim—"

"You mentioned '72. My last year with Houston. Yes, we lost the finals against Denver. Because there's a mile of elevation difference between Houston and Denver. Discs fly differently in the two cities."

He turned to the players. The young men paused in tying cleats and pulling on jerseys. "Right now, you're two miles below the elevation of the New Madison plateau. Down here, discs will fly differently than you expect. I can coach you through that. Connor, I'm sure he's a good mayor, has great amateur knowledge about ultimate, but if he coaches you today, you'll lose."

Mouths slack, Braden and most of the other players stared through wide eyes at Rambard. Lucas did too. Then he glanced at Connor and quickly turned his head.

As Mayor, Connor had long coached the team, but he could see immediately his players had already chosen their new coach. "I'd be a fool to turn down your offer," Connor said.

"You're no fool." Rambard pumped Connor's hand and slapped his back. "We're going to win this. You heard me, men?" he called to the players. "We're going to win! Hit the field!"

The players cheered and filed out of the chamber. Their cleats clattered on the regurgitated-brick floor. The sound loosened a knot of unease in Connor's gut. He had good players, and luck in having a former pro coaching them. New Madison would win this game.

Only Gonçalves remained in the room. He cleared his throat with a liquid rasp. "Mr. Little, I can't add any value to your team's play. I'll send a report now to Earth via the ansible on our ship. I'll join you on the sideline in a few minutes."

"Take your time," Connor said. "We don't need you."

Gonçalves wheezed in a breath. "A time may come to reconsider that." He waddled away.

Alone, Connor left the preparation chamber. His footsteps echoed off the chewed-and-hardened walls. Hspa Nki with thinly-beaded tails guided him to the field with sweeping gestures of their four arms.

He emerged from the tunnel into the largest enclosed space he'd ever seen on the planet. Scalloped grandstands surrounded the field, rising like the walls of an eroded canyon. Hspa Nki crowded the grandstands. Thousands of clinking alien voices echoed. *Vacuum breathers.* Connor hunched his shoulders, as if the voices were rain falling from the low gray clouds.

At the stadium's far end, a tall wall held panels with gargantuan, unreadable alien script and a twisted structure of curved, nested arms. Three Hspa Nki clung to railings under the text and structure. Connor's comm implant labeled various objects. Team names. Points. Time remaining.

Connor went to the New Madison sideline. Most of the players stretched or made short, soft warm-up throws, all with wary eyes on the steep grandstands.

"We've never played a road game before, have we?" Connor said. He squatted near the players, ran his fingers through the coiled, green-black ground cover, then beckoned for someone to throw him a disc. Though fabricated by the Hspa Nki, and as yellow as the barely-remembered sun of Earth, the weight and feel filled his hand and slotted into decades of muscle memory. "But wherever we play, it's the same field, the same disc, and the same spirit of the game."

Smiles and nods showed among the players. Braden closed his eyes and bobbed his head at some music played through his comm implant.

Rambard, Connor, and Lucas went to midfield for the opening toss. Two Hspa Nki players accompanied Nednennik, whose tail quills bore a thousand multicolored beads. Nednennik's haws peeled back and it stared at Rambard while its quills rustled.

"Good to meet you somewhere other than the negotiation chamber," Rambard said with a smirk.

Connor stepped forward. "Honored host, are all the rules clear to you and your players?"

Nednennik's voice sounded like a bag of pebbles rolled from hand to hand. "Yes," Connor's comm implant translated to his auditory nerves. "A player scores a point by catching the disc in the opponent's end zone. The possessor of the disc may not run and may only pivot on one foot and throw. The defender guarding the disc's possessor calls out ten seconds. If the possessor holds the disc for ten seconds, or throws an incomplete or intercepted pass or one landing or caught out-of-bounds, possession goes to the defending team. Contact is forbidden. Players call their own fouls, in the spirit of the game."

The humans nodded. The Hspa Nki won the toss.

Back at the human sideline, Rambard told the team, "We're throwing off. Remember! Down here, the disc won't carry as far as you're used to. Who's throwing off?"

Players nodded at Lucas. Sure hands and strong arm, a handler.

"Throw harder on the throw-off," Rambard said to him. "Trust me. It won't go for a touchback. And everyone, on deep passes, the same applies. Throw harder than you think you should. Starters, get out there!"

Braden raised his hand. "Which side do we force them to throw on?"

Since an opponent with the disc could only pivot, and most throws came sidearm, the player guarding the disc-handler would generally stand in one throwing lane to force the disc-handler to throw down the other. Announcing the forced side let defenders marking receivers know from which angle to expect a pass.

A brief frown, dispelled by a shake of Rambard's head. "They're left-handed, aren't they? Force to their left." Their forehand side.

Players nodded. The starting seven ran a couple of steps toward their own goal line.

"No!" Connor shouted.

The players stopped running and jostled together.

"Have you seen them, Rambard? They throw strong forehands. Their backhands are weak. Force to their right!"

Rambard stared at Connor, then turned to the starting seven. "As I said. Force to their left."

Connor's chest burned. Then a firm voice burst through his comm implant. "Honored guests, are you ready to begin?"

"We are," Rambard said. He slapped Braden on the shoulder. "Get out there, men!"

The players ran out to their own goal line. Lucas stood in the center and raised the disc to show his readiness. The crimson disc contrasted starkly with the blur of Hspa Nki in the far grandstand. The disc commanded the eye, like a ship at a launch station with the whole galaxy to be explored.

At the far end zone, amid a line of gray-blue figures, the tallest Hspa Nki raised its hand.

Lucas lined up for a backhand throw-off. "Game on!" He swung back his arm.

Connor's throat tightened. Too big a backswing. Rambard must have it wrong. Lucas would throw the disc through the end zone for a touchback.

Face tight, Lucas grunted and whipped his arm forward. The disc came out fast from his hand—

—and flew wrong. Too slow for the power behind it. And though discs curved a little in flight, this one banked like an airplane turning hard to the right.

Connor's stomach fell.

Rambard was correct.

The disc arced toward the right sideline and dropped through the thick air.

Hspa Nki loped toward it. Most passed it. The disc landed only a few yards beyond the center line, great field position for the aliens. The humans rushed up to play man-to-alien defense.

A Hspa Nki picked up the disc with its top left hand. Braden guarded the alien, standing in front of the alien to its right and waving his arms. Blocking its backhand passing lane, just what Rambard had called for. "One!" Braden counted. "Two!"

The Hspa Nki pivoted left and snapped a forehand pass. An effortless motion of its elbows and wrist. The disc curled over the sideline, then zipped toward a corner of the end zone. A Hspa Nki strode to the corner and raised its left hands. Lucas matched the alien stride for stride, but the disc curled inbounds past his stretching fingers.

The Hspa Nki squeezed the flying disc between its left hands. Connor's face scrunched up. Good catch, great throw.

The crowd rustled its tail quills and cheered like concrete rattling in a mixer. The human team's shoulders and heads drooped. They trudged to their goal line to receive the next point.

"Rambard!" Connor shouted. "Force to their right!"

Rambard stood stiff-backed. He lifted his palm toward Connor, yet kept his back to him, and his gaze on two players substituting in. He spoke quietly and the two players hurried onto the field.

The Hspa Nki throw-off landed three yards in front of the human goal line. Lucas made a short forehand pass to Tanner. The disc slid through the air to the left—Tanner stretched to catch it. Connor let out a breath. *The team is getting the hang of this—*

Tanner threw a backhand to Dustin. The disc curled away from Dustin and clacked into the ground. Turnover.

One Hspa Nki sprinted for the center of the end zone while a second went to the disc. A high forehand pass and the sprinting Hspa Nki caught it easily. The crowd cheered.

Cold oozed down Connor's throat.

The next human possession ended the same way, turnover and quick score. Hspa Nki 3, New Madison 0. The crowd sounded even louder this time, as if they'd thrown Connor into the mixer with the concrete.

Labored breathing suddenly cut through the noise. Gonçalves took up position next to Connor. "My regrets for my lateness. What is our situation?" He looked at the scoreboard. Hspa Nki scoreboard operators glided from perch to perch. "I see."

The world spun. Connor shut his eyes. "We're getting humiliated."

Gonçalves rested his fleshy hand on Connor's shoulder. "The game has barely begun. The winds of fortune may yet turn."

In a lull of the crowd noise, Rambard's words to the next substitutes carried to Connor. "Short passes on offense until you get a feel for the air density. On defense, force to their right! Make them beat us with their backhands!"

The Hspa Nki throw-off landed four yards in front of the end zone. Lucas picked up the disc while his teammates formed a stack, a line running toward midfield. Everyone looked more assured. One by one, human players broke from the stack to give Lucas passing opportunities. He flicked a forehand eight yards to Dustin, Dustin to Jacob past the fingertips of a lunging Hspa Nki. Back to Lucas. With more short passes, they advanced.

Braden made a sharp cut in the end zone and ran alone toward the sideline. Lucas tossed a soft forehand into the air ahead of Braden. Connor groaned. A throw that soft would drop to the ground before Braden could catch it... if they played up in New Madison. The disc seemed to levitate as Braden ran to it and cradled it in both hands.

Now, the only cheers came from the human sideline.

On the next Hspa Nki possession, the human defense forced them to their backhands. Tail quills rippled, signaling unease. The Hspa Nki backhands traveled slowly and curled off-target. One bounced off a Hspa Nki's right hands. Turnover and quick score for New Madison.

Momentum shifted for the rest of the first half. At halftime the scoreboard showed Hspa Nki 8, New Madison 6.

Connor stared at the scoreboard, looking past the players returning to the sideline. Within striking distance, but could they close the gap?

The players drank water and toweled off sweat. Rambard clapped and aimed an intense gaze at them. "Men, you're getting the hang of disc flight down here. And because you're conditioned for thinner air, you'll have stamina for the entire second half. Keep playing your game, and you'll win!"

New Madison received the throw-off to start the second half. The players sprinted to their positions. Crisp passes sliced through the thick air. Players made sharp cuts toward the disc-handler or into the corners of the end zone. On defense, they hustled to guard the disc-handler and deflected throws off their fingertips. The Hspa Nki managed several points, but with four minutes left in the game, New Madison tied the score at 13. One quick turnover later and Lucas fired a deep pass to Braden in the end zone. Connor's heart soared with the disc.

Braden caught the disc and tapped both feet a few inches inside the sideline. New Madison 14, Hspa Nki 13. Three minutes to go.

On the next throw-off, the Hspa Nki raced to the disc. Their handler launched a long but wobbly backhand toward a streaking teammate. The Hspa Nki receiver dove. Its glide membranes rippled, then air stretched them out. Its dive seemed to last forever. With its top left hand, it plucked the disc from the air an inch above the ground.

Connor's arm snapped up and his index finger jutted at the play. "Hey!"

Lucas ran up to the Hspa Nki, then swept his head from side to side. His comm implant relayed his words to the sideline. "No gliding. You agreed."

"I didn't glide," the Hspa Nki said.

"Yes, you did." Lucas pulled his arms up, as if to stretch out glide membranes.

"I didn't glide."

Lucas' face turned red. Human players ran up.

"Don't lie!"

"We all saw you glide!"

Hspa Nki huddled around their player. "She did not glide," one said.

Another alien waggled its tail quills and spoke into the ears of nearby teammates. The Hspa Nki soon argued among themselves. Rapid clattering voices and waves of rippling quills erupted, but soon died down.

Connor found himself standing next to Rambard, two yards onto the field. The Hspa Nki wouldn't blatantly cheat—

The Hspa Nki receiver set the disc on the ground, then dragged its tail quills. "Honored guest, my teammate saw my actions better than I could feel them. The disc is yours."

Lucas nodded, then looked at the still-running clock. "We're willing to add thirty seconds for this stoppage."

"What?" Rambard muttered. "Don't offer that." Thirty seconds more for the Hspa Nki to tie the score.

"That is most generous," the Hspa Nki said. "We agree."

"No!" Rambard shouted.

Connor scowled at him. "The Hspa Nki needed time to realize Lucas was right. It's in the spirit of the game to give them time back."

"We wouldn't have done that in the NAUFDL playoffs. Let alone when a human colony on this planet is at risk." Rambard clawed the air, then flung his hands forward. "Lucas offered, they agreed, we can't back out now. Damn." He retreated to the sideline.

Connor followed. His voice flowed like a wide river. "It's the spirit of the game."

"You think because I got paid to play I don't appreciate the spirit of the game?" Rambard shook his head and peered past Connor at the scoreboard. The clock stopped, ratcheted back around its spiral, then restarted.

Gaze darting between the field and Rambard, shoulders hunched, Lucas picked up the disc. "Game on!" he shouted.

Lucas' throw left his hand. The disc quickly turned over and knifed along the ground. He gaped after it.

Don't let Rambard get in your head. Just play—

The Hspa Nki formerly guarding Lucas broke toward the end zone. Mouth gaping, Lucas ran after it, but a second too slow.

Catch in the end zone. Tie game.

The next throw-off went to Lucas. A Hspa Nki with wide arms and quick feet guarded him just outside the end zone. Lucas faked a backhand, then made a soft forehand throw.

The Hspa Nki lunged for the disc. It slapped the side of the disc, keeping it spinning and deflecting it to the end zone.

Eyes wide, Lucas ran after it, shoulder to shoulder with the Hspa Nki. It stretched its top left arm toward the disc while boxing out Lucas with its right elbows. Its fingers clamped around the edge of the disc.

Connor's stomach flopped. Gonçalves' labored breath roared in his ears.

The Hspa Nki led by one.

On the next throw-off, the disc landed between Lucas and Dustin. Lucas shook his head and backed away.

Come on, Dustin, you're a good handler. Connor's thought sounded like a lie told to a child.

Three Hspa Nki raced forward, one to guard Dustin and two to stand five yards back in his passing lanes. Not a double- or triple-team, therefore legal. Dustin's head jerked around, looking for open teammates.

The guarding Hspa Nki's translated shout came through Connor's comm implant. "Eight. Nine. Te—"

Dustin tried a hammer throw to Lucas over the guarding Hspa Nki. The disc dropped like a shot bird.

Two Hspa Nki broke for opposite end zone corners. The third tossed a backhand over Lucas' outstretched hands to its teammate.

Hspa Nki 16, New Madison 14, ninety seconds to go.

Lucas hung his head. He shuffled to a stop and looked to the sideline.

"We should pull him," Rambard said.

"No," Connor said. He caught Lucas' gaze and gestured for him to calm down. "Play your game!" he shouted. To Rambard, he said, "He's the best handler we have. You've seen that?"

Rambard frowned. "That's true."

Connor filled his voice with assurance he did not feel. "Play your game!" he shouted again.

Lucas nodded at Connor, then jogged with growing intensity toward the goal line.

"Men!" yelled Rambard, "you have time to tie the game if you score quickly!"

The Hspa Nki throw-off landed three yards in front of the goal line. Lucas picked up the disc and surveyed the field. Despite the Hspa Nki guarding him, he fired a curling backhand to Jacob near midfield, then hustled up for a drop pass. He zipped a long forehand to Braden in the end zone.

Down by one. A minute to play.

Rambard sent in substitutes with fresh legs. A tie at the end of regulation would send the game to sudden death overtime. New Madison's best chance was a deep throw-off, a quickly forced turnover, and a disc to the end zone.

Lucas raised the disc in readiness. A Hspa Nki matched the gesture. Lucas threw off.

The disc headed toward the right corner in front of the Hspa Nki end zone. Connor gritted his teeth. If the disc landed over the goal line, touchback for the Hspa Nki. If it landed out of bounds, the Hspa Nki would start in the field's middle.

Braden, Quillen, and Waters raced after the disc. It landed inbounds four yards in front of the goal line. Perfect place to crowd the Hspa Nki handler.

Quillen guarded the handler, jumping from side to side and waving his arms. Braden remained five yards upfield, a foot from the sideline, blocking the forehand throwing lane. The Hspa Nki handler pivoted to forehand, to backhand—

"Seven!" Quillen counted. "Eight!"

—to forehand, and threw. Braden leaped. The disc hit his open palm and tumbled to the ground.

"Turnover!" Connor shouted.

Quillen and Waters had already broken for the end zone. The Hspa Nki player dropped back to cover Quillen heading toward the middle, leaving Waters unguarded toward the back corner. Braden picked up the disc.

Connor's breath hitched. Had Braden thrown at all today? *Come on, easy, a firm throw, float it in the thick air—*

The disc spun gently out of Braden's hand. The right throwing lane, but too soft. Like Lucas on the game's opening throw-off, he used muscle memory tuned for the thin air of New Madison. The disc glided downward, far too short for Waters to catch it in stride.

Waters' blue eyes widened. He angled back toward the disc. His cleats dug into the ground cover. The disc sank through the air. Waters stretched. Dove—

The disc clacked against the ground. It rolled on its edge over his arm and bounced into his face, then settled upside-down on the ground.

The crowd's cheers erupted. The Hspa Nki players all looked at the clock and lifted their tail quills in dominance. The human players looked too, hands on knees, eyes haggard.

Three seconds, two, one.

Zero.

The human players trudged to the sideline. Braden turned his shoulders away from his teammates. Tears flowed down his face.

"I lost the game," he said, voice choked.

Connor's arms enveloped him. "We played as a team and lost as a team."

"That's right," said Lucas, his eyes moist. Other players nodded in agreement.

Braden buried his face in Connor's shoulders. "We're going back to Earth because of me."

A labored breath heralded Gonçalves. "The winds of fortune may yet change."

Braden backed out of Connor's hug. His brows crinkled at Gonçalves. Connor glared at the lying billionaire. "Change? How?"

Gonçalves raised a palm. "I must first talk with Nednennik."

Nednennik loped across the field, glide membranes rippling. "A well-played game, honored guests," it said. "You nearly proved yourselves our equals. You must vacate our planet within thirty local days."

Older New Madisonites hadn't asked to be marooned here, but to lose the only home the young generation ever had... Connor shut his eyes. "We wi—"

"A word," Gonçalves said. "Nednennik, you told Rambard and I you would waive New Madison's land tax if we paid you ten billion dollars?"

Nednennik's tail quills flattened. "I did."

Gonçalves heaved out a breath. "I will pay it."

Connor's head swam. His comm implant caught Nednennik's skeptical reply. "You said the Exploration Consortium could not pay that amount."

"It can't. *I* can."

Rambard scowled. "What are you doing?" he hissed at Gonçalves. "Your net worth is only five billion."

"No. It *was*," Gonçalves said. "Just before the opening throw-off, I ansibled our situation to Las Vegas, on Earth. The sportsbook computers gave New Madison odds of 1:2. I wagered almost all my holdings that the Hspa Nki would win."

Nednennik writhed its quills. "New Madison would either win the game or you would pay its debt. Wisely chosen. You, of New Madison and of Earth, are truly our equals."

Amid the knot of players, Braden watched with red-rimmed eyes. His mouth parted in a newborn smile. A wave of understanding flowed from face to face.

The Hspa Nki spectators filed out of the grandstands. The scoreboard operators took down the score panels and spun back the clock's nested arms. Nednennik and the last Hspa Nki players entered the tunnel to the aliens' locker room.

Rambard stared at the coiled, green-black ground cover and shook his head.

Connor went to him. "You coached well."

"Not well enough." Rambard turned his head. "We started off forcing the wrong way—"

"You understood what the thicker air would do to the disc. I had no idea." Connor rested his arm on Rambard's shoulder. "You coached us better than I would have."

Rambard nodded yet pulled away.

Nearby, the New Madison players huddled together, again with tears. Now, though, their tears rolled down faces lifted to the sky and trickled past giddy smiles and laughing mouths.

Connor blinked at Gonçalves. For a man who barely knew them to pay so much... "You spent your entire fortune?"

"Not *entire*. I'll live comfortably enough—"

"But why? For us?" He widened his arms to indicate the players behind him.

"The Exploration Consortium will want to lease base facilities from New Madison, which benefits us both. I will win acclaim on Earth, something a fortune alone cannot buy. And a colony of human beings will keep its home of thirty years."

Pressure welled behind Connor's eyes. "Thank you."

Gonçalves shook his jowly head. "You don't need to thank me. I acted in the spirit of the game."

—The author thanks David Abmayr, Jr., Ph.D. for technical consultation regarding altitude effects on flying disc dynamics and ultimate gameplay.

About the Author

Raymund Eich files patent applications, earned a Ph.D., won a national quiz bowl championship, writes science fiction and fantasy, and affirms Robert Heinlein's dictum that specialization is for insects. In a typical day, he may talk with biochemists, electrical engineers, patent attorneys, and rocket scientists. Hundreds of papers cite his graduate research on the reactions of nitric oxide with heme proteins.

Connect with the author at **www.raymundeich.com** or scan the QR code below.

Sign up for his mailing list to receive exclusive, pre-release content about his upcoming books. Your email address will never be shared and you can unsubscribe at any time. Go to **www.raymundeich.com/mailing-list** or scan the QR code below.

Other Books by the Author

Available wherever books are sold.

Learn more about these titles at our website, **www.cv2books.com**, or scan the QR code below.

Stone Chalmers

Earth barely survived the 21st Century. Biotechnological and nuclear terrorism, civil war, famine, and ethnic cleansing killed billions. Thousands fled on warp-drive ships to colonize planets around distant suns.

In the 22nd century, after the United Nations established control over Earth, it opened wormhole links to the distant colonies, to prevent a repeat of the previous century's chaos on a galactic scale.

Enter operative Stone Chalmers. Spy. Assassin. Instrument maintaining the UN's order on the settled galaxy.

Opposing him are hostile forces on colony worlds… and within the UN itself.

When Stone clashes with those forces, the UN — and every human world — will be transformed forever.

Learn more about the Stone Chalmers series at **www.cv2books.com/stone-chalmers,** or scan the QR code below.

The Progress of Mankind (#1)

To maintain order in the 22nd century, the UN relocates undesirables through artificial wormholes onto colony planets. Everyone benefits... except the planets' original colonists.

Now, the newly rediscovered colony of New Moravia learns the UN's plan and fights back.

The Greater Glory of God (#2)

Thousands fled the chaos of the 21st century on rogue warpdrive ships to settle colony planets. When Earth reunified in the 22nd, its fleets rediscovered the colonies and hunted down the warpdrive ships.

Every warpdrive ship but one.

To All High Emprise Consecrated (#3)

After unifying Earth, the UN has rediscovered the colony of Minerva. Prosperous and technologically advanced, Minerva quickly submits to UN supremacy. Surprisingly quickly...

In Public Convocation Assembled (#4)

After unifying Earth, the UN controls all human colonies scattered through the galaxy by means of wormholes, warpdrive ships, and ruthless operatives. Operatives working to strengthen the UN.

Or destroy it.

The Confederated Worlds

The purpose of all other combat arms is to put the infantryman in sole possession of the battlefield.

A thousand years from now, while Earth sleeps in virtual reality, three polities—the Confederated Worlds, the Unity, and the Progressive Republic—strive to connect the scattered, terraformed worlds of humankind by artificial wormholes. When they meet, they clash, in a decades-long struggle of arms that will embroil every human world, in which dedication to duty liberates worlds—and oneself.

Learn more about the Confederated Worlds series at **www.cv2books.com/the-confederated-worlds**, or scan the QR code below.

Take the Shilling (Book 1)

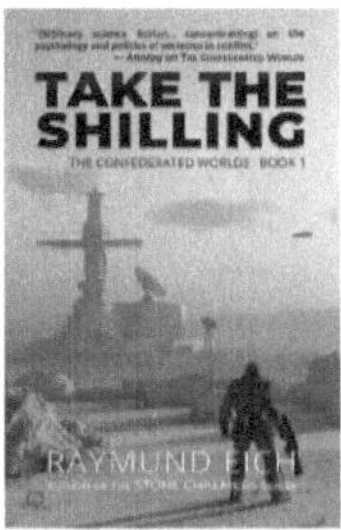

The Confederated Worlds implanted in his brain the skills to make him a soldier. Tomas Neumann had to learn for himself how to survive interstellar war.

Operation Iago (Book 2)

The Confederated Worlds lost the war. Can Lt. Tomas Neumann win the peace against elusive, deceptive foes out to turn the Confederated Worlds against itself?

A Bodyguard of Lies (Book 3)

Assigned to the halls of power, only Capt. Tomas Neumann can save the Confederated Worlds from the ultimate treachery.

Novels

The Blank Slate

Neuroscience entrepreneur Clay Shieffer must stop a tyrannical president... because he unwittingly gave the tyrant power over the human mind.

New California

After New California's founder committed suicide, two men vied to rule the colony.

Ashwin George, supported by the colony's elite and the Chinese company dominating half the settled galaxy.

Against him, Desmond Park, nanotechnology engineer, armed with the most formidable weapon of all.

A single idea.

The Reincarnation Run

Skeptical spacejock Landry Krieger knows exactly how to smuggle the "reborn" spiritual leader of an oppressed people past their conquerors... but the boy's priests—and governess—shake up his orderly plans.

Short Novels

The ALECS Quartet

He had a month to learn the planet's mysteries — and Juliette's.

His cover story: return to Elard to dismantle his sect's missionary work to the planet's natives.

His true mission: investigate decades-old mysteries of love and death.

His objective: return to Earth with his discovery.

If he can.

A Mighty Fortress

Theodore and his team from the Lutheran Interstellar Terraforming Society would transform a barren, rocky world into a refuge of faith and life.

Or die trying.

Collections

The First Voyages: The Complete Science Fiction Stories 1998-2012

From 21st century asteroid settlements to World War II Romania, from an Earth dominated by immortal aliens to Christ's empty tomb, a fresh, distinctive voice in science fiction will take you on journeys to the photosphere of the sun, the coding regions of DNA, and the complexities of the human psyche.

Stage Separations: The Complete Science Fiction Stories 2013-2018

In these pages, you can...

...race against time to solve mysteries hidden in a planet's vast desert—and in a woman's heart ...learn the true story of a president's assassination ...journey 14,000 miles to a high-tech fountain of youth ...win or go "home"—to an Earth you've never seen

and explore six other worlds created by a distinctive voice in twenty-first century science fiction.